The Adventures of the Infallible Godahl

Frederick Irving Anderson

THE ADVENTURES OF THE INFALLIBLE GODAHL

BY FREDERICK IRVING ANDERSON

1914

I
THE INFALLIBLE GODAHL

Oliver Armiston never was much of a sportsman with a rod or gun—though he could do fancy work with a pistol in a shooting gallery. He had, however, one game from which he derived the utmost satisfaction. Whenever he went traveling, which was often, he invariably caught his trains by the tip of the tail, so to speak, and hung on till he could climb aboard. In other words, he believed in close connections. He had a theory that more valuable dollars-and-cents time and good animal heat are wasted warming seats in stations waiting for trains than by missing them. The sum of joy to his methodical mind was to halt the slamming gates at the last fraction of the last second with majestic upraised hand, and to stroll aboard his parlor-car with studied deliberation, while the train crew were gnashing their teeth in rage and swearing to get even with the gateman for letting him through. Yet Mr. Armiston never missed a train. A good many of them tried to miss him, but none ever succeeded. He reckoned time and distance so nicely that it really seemed as if his trains had nothing else half so important as waiting until Mr. Oliver Armiston got aboard.

On this particular June day he was due in New Haven at two. If he failed to get there at two o'clock he could very easily arrive at three. But an hour is sixty minutes, and a minute is sixty seconds; and, further, Mr. Armiston, having passed his word that he would be there at two o'clock, surely would be.

On this particular day, by the time Armiston finally got to the Grand Central the train looked like an odds-on favorite. In the first place, he was still in his bed at an hour when another and less experienced traveler would have been watching the clock in the station waiting-room. In the second place, after kissing his wife in that absent-minded manner characteristic of true love, he became tangled in a Broadway traffic rush at the first corner. Scarcely was he extricated from this when he ran into a Socialist mass-meeting at Union Square. It was due only to the wits of his chauffeur that the taxicab was extricated with very little damage to the surrounding human scenery. But our man of method did not fret. Instead, he buried himself in his book, a treatise on Cause and Effect, which at that moment was lulling him with this soothing sentiment:

1

"There is no such thing as accident. The so-called accidents of every-day life are due to the preordained action of correlated causes, which is inevitable and over which man has no control."

This was comforting, but not much to the point, when Oliver Armiston looked up and discovered he had reached Twenty-third Street and had come to a halt. A sixty-foot truck, with an underslung burden consisting of a sixty-ton steel girder, had at this point suddenly developed weakness in its off hindwheel and settled down on the pavement across the right of way like a tired elephant. This, of course, was not an accident. It was due to a weakness in the construction of that wheel—a weakness that had from the beginning been destined to block street-cars and taxicabs at this particular spot at this particular hour.

Mr. Armiston dismounted and walked a block. Here he hailed a second taxicab and soon was spinning north again at a fair speed, albeit the extensive building operations in Fourth Avenue had made the street well-nigh impassable.

The roughness of the pavement merely shook up his digestive apparatus and gave it zest for the fine luncheon he was promising himself the minute he stepped aboard his train. His new chauffeur got lost three times in the maze of traffic about the Grand Central Station. This, however, was only human, seeing that the railroad company changed the map of Forty-second Street every twenty-four hours during the course of the building of its new terminal.

Mr. Armiston at length stepped from his taxi-cab, gave his grip to a porter and paid the driver from a huge roll of bills. This same roll was no sooner transferred back to his pocket than a nimble-fingered pickpocket removed it. This, again, was not an accident. That pickpocket had been waiting there for the last hour for that roll of bills. It was preordained, inevitable. And Oliver Armiston had just thirty seconds to catch his train by the tail and climb aboard. He smiled contentedly to himself.

It was not until he called for his ticket that he discovered his loss. For a full precious second he gazed at the hand that came away empty from his money pocket, and then:

2

"I find I left my purse at home," he said, with a grand air he knew how to assume on occasion. "My name is Mister Oliver Armiston."

Now Oliver Armiston was a name to conjure with.

"I don't doubt it," said the ticket agent dryly. "Mister Andrew Carnegie was here yesterday begging carfare to One Hundred and Twenty-fifth Street, and Mister John D. Rockefeller quite frequently drops in and leaves his dollar watch in hock. Next!"

And the ticket-agent glared at the man blocking the impatient line and told him to move on.

Armiston flushed crimson. He glanced at the clock. For once in his life he was about to experience that awful feeling of missing his train. For once in his life he was about to be robbed of that delicious sensation of hypnotizing the gatekeeper and walking majestically down that train platform that extends northward under the train-shed a considerable part of the distance toward Yonkers. Twenty seconds! Armiston turned round, still holding his ground, and glared concentrated malice at the man next in line. That man was in a hurry. In his hand he held a bundle of bills. For a second the thief-instinct that is latent in us all suggested itself to Armiston. There within reach of his hand was the money, the precious paltry dollar bills that stood between him and his train. It scared him to discover that he, an upright and honored citizen, was almost in the act of grabbing them like a common pickpocket.

Then a truly remarkable thing happened. The man thrust his handful of bills at Armiston.

"The only way I can raise this blockade is to bribe you," he said, returning Armiston's glare. "Here—take what you want—and give the rest of us a chance."

With the alacrity of a blind beggar miraculously cured by the sight of much money Armiston grabbed the handful, extracted what he needed for his ticket, and thrust the rest back into the waiting hand of his unknown benefactor. He caught the gate by a hair. So did his unknown friend. Together they walked down the platform, each matching the other's leisurely pace with his own. They might have been two potentates, so deliberately did they catch this train.

3

Armiston would have liked very much to thank this person, but the other presented so forbidding an exterior that it was hard to find a point of attack. By force of habit Armiston boarded the parlor car, quite forgetting he did not have money for a seat. So did the other. The unknown thrust a bill at the porter. "Get me two chairs," he said. "One is for this gentleman."

Once inside and settled, Armiston renewed his efforts to thank this strange person. That person took a card from his pocket and handed it to Armiston.

"Don't run away with the foolish idea," he said tartly, "that I have done you a service willingly. You were making me miss my train, and I took this means of bribing you to get you out of my way. That is all, sir. At your leisure you may send me your check for the trifle."

"A most extraordinary person!" said Armiston to himself. "Let me give you my card," he said to the other. "As to the service rendered, you are welcome to your own ideas on that. For my part I am very grateful."

The unknown took the proffered card and thrust it in his waistcoat pocket without glancing at it. He swung his chair round and opened a magazine, displaying a pair of broad unneighborly shoulders. This was rather disconcerting to Armiston, who was accustomed to have his card act as an open sesame.

"Damn his impudence!" he said to himself. "He takes me for a mendicant. I'll make copy of him!"

This was the popular author's way of getting even with those who offended his tender sensibilities.

Two things worried Armiston: One was his luncheon—or rather the absence of it; and the other was his neighbor. This neighbor, now that Armiston had a chance to study him, was a young man, well set up. He had a fine bronzed face that was not half so surly as his manner. He was now buried up to his ears in a magazine, oblivious of everything about him, even the dining-car porter, who strode down the aisle and announced the first call to lunch in the dining-car.

4

"I wonder what the fellow is reading," said Armiston to himself. He peeped over the man's shoulder and was interested at once, for the stranger was reading a copy of a magazine called by the vulgar The Whited Sepulcher. It was the pride of this magazine that no man on earth could read it without the aid of a dictionary. Yet this person seemed to be enthralled. And what was more to the point, and vastly pleasing to Armiston, the man was at that moment engrossed in one of Armiston's own effusions. It was one of his crime stories that had won him praise and lucre. It concerned the Infallible Godahl.

These stories were pure reason incarnate in the person of a scientific thief. The plot was invariably so logical that it seemed more like the output of some machine than of a human mind. Of course the plots were impossible, because the fiction thief had to be an incredible genius to carry out the details. But nevertheless they were highly entertaining, fascinating and dramatic at one and the same time.

And this individual read the story through without winking an eyelash—as though the mental effort cost him nothing—and then, to Armiston's delight, turned back to the beginning and read it again. The author threw out his chest and shot his cuffs. It was not often that such unconscious tribute fell to his lot. He took the card of his unknown benefactor. It read:

MR. J. BORDEN BENSON

The Towers

New York City

"Humph!" snorted Armiston. "An aristocrat—and a snob too!"

At this moment the aristocrat turned in his chair and handed the magazine to his companion. All his bad humor was gone.

"Are you familiar," he asked, "with this man Armiston's work? I mean these scientific thief stories that are running now."

"Ye—yes. Oh, yes," sputtered Armiston, hastily putting the other's card away. "I—in fact, you know—I take them every morning before breakfast."

In a way this was the truth, for Armiston always began his day's writing before breakfasting.

Mr. Benson smiled—a very fine smile at once boyish and sophisticated.

"Rather a heavy diet early in the morning, I should say," he replied. "Have you read this last one then?"

"Oh, yes," said the delighted author.

"What do you think of it?" asked Benson.

The author puckered his lips.

"It is on a par with the others," he said.

"Yes," said Benson thoughtfully. "I should say the same thing. And when we have said that there is nothing -left to say. They are truly a remarkable product. Quite unique, you know. And yet," he said, frowning at Armiston, "I believe that this man Armiston is to be ranked as the most dangerous man in the world to-day."

"Oh, I say—" began Armiston. But he checked himself, chuckling. He was very glad Mr. Benson had not looked at his card.

"I mean it," said the other decidedly. "And you think so yourself, I fully believe. No thinking man could do otherwise."

"In just what way? I must confess I have never thought of his work as anything but pure invention."

It was truly delicious. Armiston would certainly make copy of this person.

"I will grant," said Benson, "that there is not a thief in the world to-day clever enough—brainy enough—to take advantage of the suggestions put forth in these stories. But some day there will arise a man to whom they will be as simple as an ordinary blueprint, and he will profit accordingly. This magazine, by printing these stories, is merely furnishing him with his tools, showing him how to work. And the worst of it is—"

"Just a minute," said the author. "Agreeing for the moment that these stories will be the tools of Armiston's hero in real life some day, how about the popular magazines? They print ten such stories to one of these by Armiston."

"Ah, my friend," said Benson, "you forget one thing: The popular magazines deal with real life—the possible, the usual. And in that very thing they protect the public against sharpers, by exposing the methods of those same sharpers. But with Armiston—no. Much as I enjoy him as an intellectual treat, I am afraid—"

He didn't finish his sentence. Instead he fell to shaking his head, as though in amazement at the devilish ingenuity of the author under discussion.

"I am certainly delighted," thought that author, "that my disagreeable benefactor did not have the good grace to look at my card. This is really most entertaining." And then aloud, and treading on thin ice: "I should be very glad to tell Oliver what you say and see what he has to say about it."

Benson's face broke into a wreath of wrinkles:

"Do you know him? Well, I declare! That is a privilege. I heartily wish you would tell him."

"Would you like to meet him? I am under obligations to you. I can arrange a little dinner for a few of us."

"No," said Benson, shaking his head; "I would rather go on reading him without knowing him. Authors are so disappointing in real life. He may be some puny, anemic little half-portion, with dirty fingernails and all the rest that goes with genius. No offense to your friend! Besides, I am afraid I might quarrel with him."

"Last call for lunch in the dinin' cy—yah—aa," sang the porter. Armiston was looking at his fingernails as the porter passed. They were manicured once a day.

"Come lunch with me," said Benson heartily. "I should be pleased to have you as my guest. I apologize for being rude to you at the ticket window, but I did want to catch this train mighty bad."

Armiston laughed. "Well, you have paid my carfare," he said, "and I won't deny I am hungry enough to eat a hundred-and-ten-pound rail. I will let you buy me a meal, being penniless."

Benson arose, and as he drew out his handkerchief the card Armiston had given him fluttered into that worthy's lap. Armiston closed his hand over it, chuckling again. Fate had given him the chance of preserving his incognito with this person as long as he wished. It would be a rare treat to get him ranting again about the author Armiston.

But Armiston's host did not rant against his favorite author. In fact he was so enthusiastic over that man's genius that the same qualities which he decried as a danger to society in his opinion only added luster to the work. Benson asked his guest innumerable questions as to the personal qualities of his ideal, and Armiston shamelessly constructed a truly remarkable person. The other listened entranced.

"No, I don't want to know him," he said. "In the first place I haven't the time, and in the second I'd be sure to start a row. And then there is another thing: If he is half the man I take him to be from what you say, he wouldn't stand for people fawning on him and telling him what a wonder he is. That's about what I should be doing, I am afraid."

"Oh," said Armiston, "he isn't so bad as that. He is a—well, a sensible chap, with clean fingernails and all that, you know, and he gets a haircut once every three weeks, the same as the rest of us."

"I am glad to hear you say so, Mister—er—"

Benson fell to chuckling.

"By gad," he said, "here we have been talking with each other for an hour, and I haven't so much as taken a squint at your card to see who you are!"

He searched for the card Armiston had given him.

"Call it Brown," said Armiston, lying gorgeously and with a feeling of utmost righteousness. "Martin Brown, single, read-and-write, color white, laced shoes and derby hat, as the police say."

"All right, Mr. Brown; glad to know you. We will have some cigars. You have no idea how much you interest me, Mr. Brown. How much does Armiston get for his stories?"

"Every word he writes brings him the price of a good cigar. I should say he makes forty thousand a year."

"Humph! That is better than Godahl, his star creation, could bag as a thief, I imagine, let alone the danger of getting snipped with a pistol ball on a venture."

Armiston puffed up his chest and shot his cuffs again.

"How does he get his plots?"

Armiston knitted his ponderous brows. "There's the rub," he said. "You can talk about so-and-so much a word until you are deaf, dumb and blind. But, after all, it isn't the number of words or how they are strung together that makes a story. It is the ideas. And ideas are scarce."

"I have an idea that I have always wanted to have Armiston get hold of, just to see what he could do with it. If you will pardon me, to my way of thinking the really important thing isn't the ideas, but how to work out the details."

"What's your idea?" asked Armiston hastily. He was not averse to appropriating anything he encountered in real life and dressing it up to suit his taste. "I'll pass it on to Armiston, if you say so."

"Will you? That's capital. To begin with," Mr. Benson said as he twirled his brandy glass with long, lean, silky fingers—a hand Armiston thought he would not like to have handle him in a rage— "To begin with, Godahl, this thief, is not an ordinary thief, he is a highbrow. He has made some big hauls. He must be a very rich man now—eh? You see that he is quite real to me. By this time, I should say, Godahl has acquired such a fortune that thieving for mere money is no longer an object. What does he do? Sit down and live on

9

his income? Not much. He is a person of refined tastes with an eye for the esthetic. He desires art objects, rare porcelains, a gem of rare cut or color set by Benvenuto Cellini, a Leonardo da Vinci—did Godahl steal the Mona Lisa, by the way? He is the most likely person I can think of—or perhaps a Gutenberg Bible. Treasures, things of exquisite beauty to look at, to enjoy in secret, not to show to other people. That is the natural development of this man Godahl, eh?"

"Splendid!" exclaimed Armiston, his enthusiasm getting the better of him.

"Have you ever heard of Mrs. Billy Wentworth?" asked Benson.

"Indeed, I know her well," said Armiston, his guard down.

"Then you must surely have seen her white ruby?"

"White ruby! I never heard of such a thing. A white ruby?"

"Exactly. That's just the point. Neither have I. But if Godahl heard of a white ruby the chances are he would possess it—especially if it were the only one of its kind in the world."

"Gad! I do believe he would, from what I know of him."

"And especially," went on Benson, "under the circumstances. You know the Wentworths have been round a good deal. They haven't been overscrupulous in getting things they wanted. Now Mrs. Wentworth—but before I go on with this weird tale I want you to understand me. It is pure fiction—an idea for Armiston and his wonderful Godahl. I am merely suggesting the Wentworths as fictitious characters."

"I understand," said Armiston.

"Mrs. Wentworth might very well possess this white ruby. Let us say she stole it from some potentate's household in the Straits Settlements. She gained admittance by means of the official position of her husband. They can't accuse her of theft. All they can do is to steal the gem back from her. It is a sacred stone of course. They always are in fiction stories. And the usual tribe of jugglers, rug-peddlers, and so on—all disguised, you understand—have followed her to America, seeking a chance, not on her life, not to commit violence of any kind, but to steal that stone.

"She can't wear it," went on Benson. "All she can do is to hide it away in some safe place. What is a safe place? Not a bank. Godahl could crack a bank with his little finger. So might those East Indian fellows laboring under the call of religion. Not in a safe. That would be folly."

"How then?" put in Armiston eagerly.

"Ah, there you are! That's for Godahl to find out. He knows, let us say, that these foreigners in one way or another have turned Mrs. Wentworth's apartments upside down. They haven't found anything. He knows that she keeps that white ruby in that house. Where is it? Ask Godahl. Do you see the point? Has Godahl ever cracked a nut like that? No. Here he must be the cleverest detective in the world and the cleverest thief at the same time. Before he can begin thieving he must make his blueprints.

"When I read Armiston," continued Benson, "that is the kind of problem that springs up in my mind. I am always trying to think of some knot this wonderful thief would have to employ his best powers to unravel. I think of some weird situation like this one. I say to myself: 'Good! I will write that. I will be as famous as Armiston. I will create another Godahl.' But," he said with a wave of his hands, "what is the result? I tie the knot, but I can't untie it. The trouble is, I am not a Godahl. And this man Armiston, as I read him, is Godahl. He must be, or else Godahl could not be made to do the wonderful things he does. Hello! New Haven already? Mighty sorry to have you go, old chap. Great pleasure. When you get to town let me know. Maybe I will consent to meet Armiston."

Armiston's first care on returning to New York was to remember the providential loan by which he had been able to keep clean his record of never missing a train. He counted out the sum in bills, wrote a polite note, signed it "Martin Brown," and dispatched it by messenger boy to J. Borden Benson, The Towers. The Towers, the address Mr. Benson's card bore, is an ultra-fashionable apartment hotel in lower Fifth Avenue. It maintains all the pomp and solemnity of an English ducal castle. Armiston remembered having on a remote occasion taken dinner there with a friend, and the recollection always gave him a chill. It was like dining among ghosts of kings, so grand and funereal was the air that pervaded everything.

Armiston, who could not forbear curiosity as to his queer benefactor, took occasion to look him up in the Blue Book and the Club Directory, and found that J. Borden Benson was quite some personage, several lines being devoted to him. This was extremely pleasing. Armiston had been thinking of that white-ruby yarn. It appealed to his sense of the dramatic. He would work it up in his best style, and on publication have a fine laugh on Benson by sending him an autographed copy and thus waking that gentleman up to the fact that it really had been the great Armiston in person he had befriended and entertained. What a joke it would be on Benson, thought the author; not without an intermixture of personal vanity, for even a genius such as he was not blind to flattery properly applied, and Benson unknowingly had laid it on thick.

"And, by gad!" thought the author, "I will use the Wentworths as the main characters, as the victims of Godahl. They are just the people to fit into such a romance. Benson put money in my pocket, though he didn't suspect it. Lucky he didn't know what shifts we popular authors are put to for plots."

Suiting the action to the words, Armiston and his wife accepted the next invitation they received from the Wentworths.

Mrs. Wentworth, be it understood, was a lion hunter. She was forever trying to gather about her such celebrities as Armiston the author, Brackens the painter, Johanssen the explorer, and others. Armiston had always withstood her wiles. He always had some excuse to keep him away from her gorgeous table, where she exhibited her lions to her simpering friends.

There were many undesirables sitting at the table, idle-rich youths, girls of the fast hunting set, and so on, and they all gravely shook the great author by the hand and told him what a wonderful man he was. As for Mrs. Wentworth, she was too highly elated at her success in roping him for sane speech, and she fluttered about him like a hysterical bridesmaid. But, Armiston noted with relief, one of his pals was there—Johanssen. Over cigars and cognac he managed to buttonhole the explorer.

"Johanssen," he said, "you have been everywhere."

"You are mistaken there," said Johanssen. "I have never before tonight been north of Fifty-ninth Street in New York."

"Yes, but you have been in Java and Ceylon and the Settlements. Tell me, have you ever heard of such a thing as a white ruby?"

The explorer narrowed his eyes to a slit and looked queerly at his questioner. "That's a queer question," he said in a low voice, "to ask in this house."

Armiston felt his pulse quicken. "Why?" he asked, assuming an air of surprised innocence.

"If you don't know," said the explorer shortly, "I certainly will not enlighten you."

"All right; as you please. But you haven't answered my question yet. Have you ever heard of a white ruby?"

"I don't mind telling you that I have heard of such a thing—that is, I have heard there is a ruby in existence that is called the white ruby. It isn't really white, you know; it has a purplish tinge. But the old heathen who rightly owns it likes to call it white, just as he likes to call his blue and gray elephants white."

"Who owns it?" asked Armiston, trying his best to make his voice sound natural. To find in this manner that there was some parallel for the mystical white ruby of which Benson had told him appealed strongly to his super-developed dramatic sense. He was now as keen on the scent as a hound.

Johanssen took to drumming on the tablecloth. He smiled to himself and his eyes glowed. Then he turned and looked sharply at his questioner.

"I suppose," he said, "that all things are grist to a man of your trade. If you are thinking of building a story round a white ruby I can think of nothing more fascinating. But, Armiston," he said, suddenly altering his tone and almost whispering, "if you are on the track of *the* white ruby let me advise you now to call off your dogs and keep your throat whole. I think I am a brave man. I have shot tigers at ten paces—held my fire purposely to see how charmed a life I really did bear. I have been charged by mad rhinos and by wounded buffaloes. I have walked across a clearing where the air was being punctured with bullets as thick as holes in a mosquito screen. But," he said, laying his hand on Armiston's arm, "I have never had the nerve to hunt the white ruby."

"Capital!" exclaimed the author.

"Capital, yes, for a man who earns his bread and gets his excitement by sitting at a typewriter and dreaming about these things. But take my word for it, it isn't capital for a man who gets his excitement by doing this thing. Hands off, my friend!"

"It really does exist then?"

Johanssen puckered his lips. "So they say," he said.

"What's it worth?"

"Worth? What do you mean by worth? Dollars and cents? What is your child worth to you? A million, a billion—how much? Tell me. No, you can't. Well, that's just what this miserable stone is worth to the man who rightfully owns it. Now let's quit talking nonsense. There's Billy Wentworth shooing the men into the drawing-room. I suppose we shall be entertained this evening by some of the hundred-dollar-a-minute songbirds, as usual. It's amazing what these people will spend for mere vulgar display when there are hundreds of families starving within a mile of this spot!"

Two famous singers sang that night. Armiston did not have much opportunity to look over the house. He was now fully determined to lay the scene of his story in this very house. At leave-taking the sugar-sweet Mrs. Billy Wentworth drew Armiston aside and said:

"It's rather hard on you to ask you to sit through an evening with these people. I will make amends by asking you to come to me some night when we can be by ourselves. Are you interested in rare curios? Yes, we all are. I have some really wonderful things I want you to see. Let us make it next Tuesday, with a little informal dinner, just for ourselves."

Armiston then and there made the lion hunter radiantly happy by accepting her invitation to sit at her board as a family friend instead of as a lion.

As he put his wife into their automobile he turned and looked at the house. It stood opposite Central Park. It was a copy of some French chateau in gray sandstone, with a barbican, and overhanging towers, and all the rest of it. The windows of the street floor peeped out through deep embrasures and were heavily guarded with iron latticework.

"Godahl will have the very devil of a time breaking in there," he chuckled to himself. Late that night his wife awakened him to find out why he was tossing about so.

"That white ruby has got on my nerves," he said cryptically, and she, thinking he was dreaming, persuaded him to try to sleep again.

Great authors must really live in the flesh, at times at least, the lives of their great characters. Otherwise these great characters would not be so real as they are. Here was Armiston, who had created a superman in the person of Godahl the thief. For ten years he had written nothing else. He had laid the life of Godahl out in squares, thought for him, dreamed about him, set him to new tasks, gone through all sorts of queer adventures with him. And this same Godahl had amply repaid him. He had raised the author from the ranks of struggling amateurs to a position among the most highly paid fiction writers in the United States. He had brought him ease and luxury. Armiston did not need the money any more. The serial rights telling of the exploits of this Godahl had paid him handsomely. The books of Godahl's adventures had paid him even better, and had furnished him yearly with a never-failing income, like government bonds, but at a much higher rate of interest. Even though the crimes this Godahl had committed were all on paper and almost impossible, nevertheless Godahl was a living being to his creator. More—he was Armiston, and Armiston was Godahl.

It was not surprising, then, that when Tuesday came Armiston awaited the hour with feverish impatience. Here, as his strange friend had so thoughtlessly and casually told him was an opportunity for the great Godahl to outdo even himself. Here was an opportunity for Godahl to be the greatest detective in the world, in the first place, before he could carry out one of his sensational thefts.

So it was Godahl, not Armiston, who helped his wife out of their automobile that evening and mounted the splendid steps of the Wentworth mansion. He cast his eye aloft, took in every inch of the facade.

"No," he said, "Godahl cannot break in from the street. I must have a look at the back of the house."

He cast his eyes on the ironwork that guarded the deep windows giving on the street.

It was not iron after all, but chilled steel sunk into armored concrete. The outposts of this house were as safely guarded as the vault of the United States mint.

"It's got to be from the inside," he said, making mental note of this fact.

The butler was stone-deaf. This was rather singular. Why should a family of the standing of the Wentworths employ a man as head of their city establishment who was stone-deaf? Armiston looked at the man with curiosity. He was still in middle age. Surely, then, he was not retained because of years of service. No, there was something more than charity behind this. He addressed a casual word to the man as he handed him his hat and cane. His back was turned and the man did not reply. Armiston turned and repeated the sentence in the same tone. The man watched his lips in the bright light of the hall.

"A lip-reader, and a dandy," thought Armiston, for the butler seemed to catch every word he said.

"Fact number two!" said the creator of Godahl the thief.

He felt no compunction at thus noting the most intimate details of the Wentworth establishment. An accident had put him on the track of a rare good story, and it was all copy. Besides, he told himself, when he came to write the story he would disguise it in such a way that no one reading it would know it was about the Wentworths. If their establishment happened to possess the requisite setting for a great story, surely there was no reason why he should not take advantage of that fact.

The great thief—he made no bones of the fact to himself that he had come here to help Godahl—accepted the flattering greeting of his hostess with the grand air that so well fitted him. Armiston was tall and thin, with slender fingers and a touch of gray in his wavy hair, for all his youthful years, and he knew how to wear his clothes. Mrs. Wentworth was proud of him as a social ornament, even aside from his glittering fame as an author. And Mrs. Armiston was well born, so there was no jar in their being received in the best house of the town.

The dinner was truly delightful. Here Armiston saw, or thought he saw, one of the reasons for the deaf butler. The hostess had him so trained that she was able to catch her servant's eye and instruct him in this or that trifle by merely moving her lips. It was almost uncanny, thought the author, this silent conversation the deaf man and his mistress were able to carry on unnoticed by the others.

"By gad, it's wonderful! Godahl, my friend, underscore that note of yours referring to the deaf butler. Don't miss it. It will take a trick."

Armiston gave his undivided attention to his hostess as soon as he found Wentworth entertaining Mrs. Armiston and thus properly dividing the party. He persuaded her to talk by a cleverly pointed question here and there; and as she talked, he studied her.

"We are going to rob you of your precious white ruby, my friend," he thought humorously to himself; "and while we are laying our wires there is nothing about you too small to be worthy of our attention."

Did she really possess the white ruby? Did this man Benson know anything about the white ruby? And what was the meaning of the strange actions of his friend Johanssen when approached on the subject in this house? His hostess came to have a wonderful fascination for him. He pictured this beautiful creature so avid in her lust for rare gems that she actually did penetrate the establishment of some heathen potentate in the Straits simply for the purpose of stealing the mystic stone. "Have you ever, by any chance, been in the Straits?" he asked indifferently.

"Wait," Mrs. Wentworth said with a laugh as she touched his hand lightly; "I have some curios from the Straits, and I will venture to say you have never seen their like."

Half an hour later they were all seated over coffee and cigarettes in Mrs. Wentworth's boudoir. It was indeed a strange place. There was scarcely a single corner of the world that had not contributed something to its furnishing. Carvings of teak and ivory; hangings of sweet-scented vegetable fibers; lamps of jade; queer little gods, all sitting like Buddha with their legs drawn up under them, carved out of jade or sardonyx; scarfs of baroque pearls; Darjeeling turquoises— Armiston had never before seen such a collection. And each item had its story. He began to look on this frail little woman with different eyes. She had been and seen and done, and the tale of her life, what she had actually lived, outshone even that of the glittering rascal Godahl, who was standing beside him now and directing his ceaseless questions. "Have you any rubies?" he asked.

Mrs. Wentworth bent before a safe in the wall. With swift fingers she whirled the combination. The keen eyes of Armiston followed the bright knob like a cat.

"Fact number three!" said the Godahl in him as he mentally made note of the numbers. "Five—eight—seven—four—six. That's the combination."

Mrs. Wentworth showed him six pigeon-blood rubies. "This one is pale," he said carelessly, holding a particularly large stone up to the light. "Is it true that occasionally they are found white?"

His hostess looked at him before answering. He was intent on a deep-red stone he held in the palm of his hand. It seemed a thousand miles deep.

"What a fantastic idea!" she said. She glanced at her husband, who had reached out and taken her hand in a naturally affectionate manner.

"Fact number four!" mentally noted Armiston. "Are not you in mortal fear of robbery with all of this wealth?"

Mrs. Wentworth laughed lightly.

"That is why we live in a fortress," she said.

"Have you never, then, been visited by thieves?" asked the author boldly.

"Never!" she said.

"A lie," thought Armiston. "Fact number five! We are getting on swimmingly."

"I do not believe that even your Godahl the Infallible could get in here," Mrs. Wentworth said. "Not even the servants enter this room. That door is not locked with a key; yet it locks. I am not much of a housekeeper," she said lazily, "but such housekeeping as is done in this room is all done by these poor little hands of mine."

"No! Most amazing! May I look at the door?"

"Yes, Mr. Godahl," said this woman, who had lived more lives than Godahl himself.

Armiston examined the door, this strange device that locked without a key, apparently indeed without a lock, and came away disappointed.

"Well, Mr. Godahl?" his hostess said tauntingly. He shook his head in perplexity.

"Most ingenious," he said; and then suddenly: "Yet I will venture that if I turned Godahl loose on this problem he would solve it."

"What fun!" she cried clapping her hands.

"You challenge him?" asked Armiston.

"What nonsense is this!" cried Wentworth, coming forward.

"No nonsense at all," said Mrs. Wentworth. "Mr. Armiston has just said that his Godahl could rob me. Let him try. If he can—if mortal man can gain the secret of ingress and egress of this room—I want to know it. I don't believe mortal man can enter this room."

Armiston noted a strange glitter in her eyes.

"Gad! She was born to the part! What a woman!" he thought. And then aloud:

"I will set him to work. I will lay the scene of his exploit in—say—Hungary, where this room might very well exist in some feudal castle. How many people have entered this room since it was made the storehouse of all this wealth?"

"Not six besides yourself," replied Mrs. Wentworth.

"Then no one can recognize it if I describe it in a story—in fact, I will change the material details. We will say that it is not jewels Godahl is seeking. We will say that it is a—"

Mrs. Wentworth's hand touched his own. The tips of her fingers were cold. "A white ruby," she said.

"Gad! What a thoroughbred!" he exclaimed to himself—or to Godahl. And then aloud: "Capital! I will send you a copy of the story autographed."

The next day he called at The Towers and sent up his card to Mr. Benson's apartments. Surely a man of Benson's standing could be trusted with such a secret. In fact it was evidently not a secret to Benson, who in all probability was one of the six Mrs. Wentworth said had entered that room. Armiston wanted to talk the matter over with Benson. He had given up his idea of having fun with him by sending him a marked copy of the magazine containing his tale. His story had taken complete possession of him, as always had been the case when he was at work dispatching Godahl on his adventures.

"If that ruby really exists," Armiston said, "I don't know whether I shall write the story or steal the ruby for myself. Benson is right. Godahl should not steal any more for mere money. He is after rare, unique things now. And I am Godahl. I feel the same way myself."

A valet appeared, attired in a gorgeous livery. Armiston wondered why any self-respecting American would consent to don such raiment, even though it was the livery of the great Benson family.

"Mr. Armiston, sir," said the valet, looking at the author's card he held in his hand. "Mr. Benson sailed for Europe yesterday morning. He is spending the summer in Norway. I am to follow on the next steamer. Is there any message I can take to him, sir? I have heard him speak of you, sir."

Armiston took the card and wrote on it in pencil:

"I called to apologize. I am Martin Brown. The chance was too good to miss. You will pardon me, won't you?"

For the next two weeks Armiston gave himself over to his dissipation, which was accompanying Godahl on this adventure. It was a formidable task. The secret room he placed in a Hungarian castle, as he had promised. A beautiful countess was his heroine. She had seen the world, mostly in man's attire, and her escapades had furnished vivacious reading for two continents. No one could possibly connect her with Mrs. Billy Wentworth. So far it was easy. But how was Godahl to get into this wonderful room where the countess had hidden this wonderful rare white ruby? The room was lined with chilled steel. Even the door—this he had noted when he was examining that peculiar portal—was lined with layers of steel. It could withstand any known tool.

However, Armiston was Armiston, and Godahl was Godahl. He got into that room. He got the white ruby!

The manuscript went to the printers, and the publishers said that Armiston had never done anything like it since he started Godahl on his astonishing career.

He banked the check for his tale, and as he did so he said: "Gad! I would a hundred times rather possess that white ruby. Confound the thing! I feel as if I had not heard the last of it."

Armiston and his wife went to Maine for the summer without leaving their address. Along in the early fall he received by registered mail, forwarded by his trusted servant at the town house, a package containing the envelope he had addressed to J. Borden Benson, The Towers. Furthermore it contained the dollar bills he had dispatched to that individual, together with his note which he had signed "Martin Brown." And across the note, in the most insulting manner, was written in coarse, greasy blue-pencil lines:

"Damnable impertinence. I'll cane you the first time I see you."

And no more. That was enough of course—quite sufficient.

In the same mail came a note from Armiston's publishers, saying that his story, The White Ruby, was scheduled for publication in the October number, out September twenty-fifth. This cheered him up. He was anxious to see it in print. Late in September they started back to town.

"Aha!" he said as he sat reading his paper in the parlor car,—he had caught this train by the veriest tip of its tail and upset the running schedule in the act—"Ah! I see my genial friend, J. Borden Benson, is in town, contrary to custom at this time of year. Life must be a great bore to that snob."

A few days after arriving in town he received a package of advance copies of the magazine containing his story, and he read the tale of The White Ruby as if he had never seen it before. On the cover of one copy, which he was to dispatch to his grumpy benefactor, J. Borden Benson, he wrote:

Charmed to be caned. Call any time. See contents.

Oliver Armiston.

On another he wrote:

Dear Mrs. Wentworth: See how simple it is to pierce your fancied security!

He dispatched these two magazines with a feeling of glee. No sooner had he done so, however, than he learned that the Wentworths had not yet returned from Newport. The magazine would be forwarded to them no doubt. The Wentworths' absence made the tale all the better, in fact, for in his story Armiston had insisted on Godahl's breaking into the castle and solving the mystery of the keyless door during the season when the chateau was closed and strung with a perfect network of burglar alarms connecting with the *gendarmerie* in the near-by village.

That was the twenty-fifth day of September. The magazine was put on sale that morning.

On the twenty-sixth day of September Armiston bought a late edition of an afternoon paper from a leather-lunged boy who was hawking "Extra!" in the street. Across the first page the headlines met his eye:

ROBBERY AND MURDER IN THE WENTWORTH MANSION!

Private watchmen, summoned by burglar alarm at ten o'clock this morning, find servant with skull crushed on floor of mysterious steel-doored room. Murdered man's pockets filled with rare jewels. Police believe he was murdered by confederate who escaped.

The Wentworth Butler, Stone Deaf, Had Just Returned From Newport To Open House At Time Of Murder.

It was ten o'clock that night when an automobile drew up at Armiston's door and a tall man with a square jaw, square shoes and a square mustache alighted. This was Deputy Police Commissioner Byrnes, a professional detective whom the new administration had drafted into the city's service from the government secret service.

Byrnes was admitted, and as he advanced to the middle of the drawing-room, without so much as a nod to the ghostlike Armiston who stood shivering before him, he drew a package of papers from his pocket.

"I presume you have seen all the evening papers," he said, spitting his words through his half-closed teeth with so much show of personal malice that Armiston—never a brave man in spite of his Godahl—cowered before him.

Armiston shook his head dumbly at first, but at length he managed to say: "Not all; no."

The deputy commissioner with much deliberation drew out the latest extra and handed it to Armiston without a word.

It was the Evening News. The first page was divided down its entire length by a black line. On one side and occupying four columns, was a word-for-word reprint of Armiston's story, The White Ruby.

On the other, the facts in deadly parallel, was a graphic account of the robbery and murder at the home of Billy Wentworth. The parallel was glaring in the intensity of its dumb accusation. On the one side was the theoretical Godahl, working his masterly way of crime, step by step; and on the other was the plagiarism of Armiston's story, following the intricacies of the master mind with copybook accuracy.

The editor, who must have been a genius in his way, did not accuse. He simply placed the fiction and the fact side by side and let the reader judge for himself. It was masterly. If, as the law says, the mind that conceives, the intelligence that directs, a crime is more guilty than the very hand that acts, then Armiston here was both thief and murderer. Thief, because the white ruby had actually been stolen. Mrs. Billy Wentworth, rushed to the city by special train, attended by doctors and nurses, now confirmed the story of the theft of the ruby. Murderer, because in the story Godahl had for once in his career stooped to murder as the means, and had triumphed over the dead body of his confederate, scorning, in his joy at possessing the white ruby, the paltry diamonds, pearls and red rubies with which his confederate had crammed his pockets.

Armiston seized the police official by his lapels.

"The butler!" he screamed. "The butler! Yes, the butler. Quick, or he will have flown."

Byrnes gently disengaged the hands that had grasped him.

"Too late," he said. "He has already flown. Sit down and quiet your nerves. We need your help. You are the only man in the world who can help us now."

When Armiston was himself again he told the whole tale, beginning with his strange meeting with J. Borden Benson on the train, and ending with his accepting Mrs. Wentworth's challenge to have Godahl break into the room and steal the white ruby. Byrnes nodded over the last part. He had already heard that from Mrs. Wentworth, and there was the autographed copy of the magazine to show for it.

"You say that J. Borden Benson told you of this white ruby in the first place."

Armiston again told, in great detail, the circumstances, all the humor now turned into grim tragedy.

"That is strange," said the ex-secret-service chief. "Did you leave your purse at home or was your pocket picked?"

"I thought at first that I had absent-mindedly left it at home. Then I remembered having paid the chauffeur out of the roll of bills, so my pocket must have been picked."

"What kind of a looking man was this Benson?"

"You must know him," said Armiston.

"Yes, I know him; but I want to know what he looked like to you. I want to find out how he happened to be so handy when you were in need of money."

Armiston described the man minutely.

The deputy sprang to his feet. "Come with me," he said; and they hurried into the automobile and soon drew up in front of The Towers.

Five minutes later they were ushered into the magnificent apartment of J. Borden Benson. That worthy was in his bath preparing to retire for the night.

"I don't catch the name," Armiston and the deputy heard him cry through the bathroom door to his valet.

"Mr. Oliver Armiston, sir."

"Ah, he has come for his caning, I expect. I'll be there directly."

He did not wait to complete his toilet, so eager was he to see the author. He strode out in a brilliant bathrobe and in one hand he carried an alpenstock. His eyes glowed in anger. But the sight of Byrnes surprised as well as halted him.

"Do you mean to say this is J. Borden Benson?" cried Armiston to Byrnes, rising to his feet and pointing at the man.

"The same," said the deputy; "I swear to it. I know him well! I take it he is not the gentleman who paid your carfare to New Haven."

"Not by a hundred pounds!" exclaimed Armiston as he surveyed the huge bulk of the elephantine clubman.

The forced realization that the stranger he had hitherto regarded as a benefactor was not J. Borden Benson at all, but some one who had merely assumed that worthy's name while he was playing the conceited author as an easy dupe, did more to quiet Armiston's nerves than all the sedatives his doctor had given him. It was a badly dashed popular author who sat down with the deputy commissioner in his library an hour later. He would gladly have consigned Godahl to the bottom of the sea; but it was too late. Godahl had taken the trick.

"How do you figure it?" Armiston asked, turning to the deputy.

"The beginning is simple enough. It is the end that bothers me," said the official. "Your bogus J. Borden Benson is, of course, the brains of the whole combination. Your infernal Godahl has told us just exactly how this crime was committed. Now your infernal Godahl must bring the guilty parties to justice."

It was plain to be seen that the police official hated Godahl worse than poison, and feared him too.

"Why not look in the Rogues' Gallery for this man who befriended me on the train?"

The chief laughed.

"For the love of Heaven, Armiston, do you, who pretend to know all about scientific thievery, think for a moment that the man who took your measure so easily is of the class of crooks who get their pictures in the Rogues' Gallery? Talk sense!"

"I can't believe you when you say he picked my pocket."

"I don't care whether you believe me or not; he did, or one of his pals did. It all amounts to the same thing, don't you see? First, he wanted to get acquainted with you. Now the best way to get into your good graces was to put you unsuspectingly under obligation to him. So he robs you of your money. From what I have seen of you in the last few hours it must have been like taking candy from a child. Then he gets next to you in line. He pretends that you are merely some troublesome toad in his path. He gives you money for your ticket, to get you out of his way so he won't miss his train. His train! Of course his train is your train. He puts you in a position where you have to make advances to him. And then, grinning to himself all the time at your conceit and gullibility, he plays you through your pride, your Godahl. Think of the creator of the great Godahl falling for a trick like that!"

Byrnes' last words were the acme of biting sarcasm.

"You admit yourself that he is too clever for you to put your hands on."

"And then," went on Byrnes, not heeding the interruption, "he invites you to lunch and tells you what he wants you to do for him. And you follow his lead like a sheep at the tail of the bellwether! Great Scott, Armiston! I would give a year's salary for one hour's conversation with that man."

Armiston was beginning to see the part this queer character had played; but he was in a semi-hysterical state, and, like a woman in such a position, he wanted a calm mind to tell him the whole thing in words of one syllable, to verify his own dread.

"What do you mean?" he asked. "I don't quite follow. You say he tells me what he wants me to do."

Byrnes shrugged his shoulders in disgust; then, as if resigned to the task before him, he began his explanation:

"Here, man, I will draw a diagram for you. This gentleman friend of yours—we will call him John Smith for convenience—wants to get possession of this white ruby. He knows that it is in the keeping of Mrs. Billy Wentworth. He knows you know Mrs. Wentworth and have access to her house. He knows that she stole this bauble and is frightened to death all the time. Now John Smith is a pretty clever chap. He handled the great Armiston like hot putty. He had exhausted his resources. He is baffled and needs help. What does he do? He reads the stories about the great Godahl. Confidently, Mr. Armiston, I will tell you that I think your great Godahl is mush. But that is neither here nor there. If you can sell him as a gold brick, all right. But Mr. John Smith is struck by the wonderful ingenuity of this Godahl. He says: 'Ha! I will get Godahl to tell me how to get this gem!'

"So he gets hold of yourself, sir, and persuades you that you are playing a joke on him by getting him to rant and rave about the great Godahl. Then—and here the villain enters—he says: 'Here is a thing the great Godahl cannot do. I dare him to do it.' He tells you about the gem, whose very existence is quite fantastic enough to excite the imagination of the wonderful Armiston. And by clever suggestion he persuades you to lay the plot at the home of Mrs. Wentworth. And all the time you are chuckling to yourself, thinking what a rare joke you are going to have on J. Borden Benson when you send him an autographed copy and show him that he was talking to the distinguished genius all the time and didn't know it. That's the whole story, sir. Now wake up!"

Byrnes sat back in his chair and regarded Armiston with the smile a pedagogue bestows on a refractory boy whom he has just flogged soundly.

"I will explain further," he continued. "You haven't visited the house yet. You can't. Mrs. Wentworth, for all she is in bed with four dozen hot-water bottles, would tear you limb from limb if you went there. And don't you think for a minute she isn't able to. That woman is a vixen."

Armiston nodded gloomily. The very thought of her now sent him into a cold sweat.

"Mr. Godahl, the obliging," continued the deputy, "notes one thing to begin with: The house cannot be entered from the outside. So it must be an inside job. How can this be accomplished? Well, there is the deaf butler. Why is he deaf? Godahl ponders. Ha! He has it! The Wentworths are so dependent on servants that they must have them round at all times. This butler is the one who is constantly about them. They are worried to death by their possession of this white ruby. Their house has been raided from the inside a dozen times. Nothing is taken, mind you. They suspect their servants. This thing haunts them, but the woman will not give up this foolish bauble. So she has as her major domo a man who cannot understand a word in any language unless he is looking at the speaker and is in a bright light. He can only understand the lips. Handy, isn't it? In a dull light or with their backs turned they can talk about anything they want to. This is a jewel of a butler.

"But," added Byrnes, "one day a man calls. He is a lawyer. He tells the butler he is heir to a fortune—fifty thousand dollars. He must go to Ireland to claim it. Your friend on the train—he is the man of course—sends your butler to Ireland. So this precious butler is lost. They must have another. Only a deaf one will do. And they find just the man they want—quite accidentally, you understand. Of course it is Godahl, with forged letters saying he has been in service in great houses. Presto! The great Godahl himself is now the butler. It is simple enough to play deaf. You say this is fiction. Let me tell you this: Six weeks ago the Wentworths actually changed butlers. That hasn't come out in the papers yet."

Armiston, who had listened to the deputy's review of his story listlessly, now sat up with a start. He suddenly exclaimed gleefully:

"But my story didn't come out till two days ago!"

"Ah, yes; but you forget that it has been in the hands of your publishers for three months. A man who was clever enough to dupe the great Armiston wouldn't shirk the task of getting hold of a proof of that story."

Armiston sank deeper into his chair.

"Once Godahl got inside the house the rest was simple. He corrupted one of the servants. He opened the steel-lined door with the flame of an oxyacetylene blast. As you say in your story that flame cuts steel like wax; he didn't have to bother about the lock. He simply cut the door down. Then he put his confederate in good humor by telling him to fill his pockets with the diamonds and other junk in the safe, which he obligingly opens. One thing bothers me, Armiston. How did you find out about that infernal contraption that killed the confederate?"

Armiston buried his face in his hands. Byrnes rudely shook him.

"Come," he said; "you murdered that man, though you are innocent. Tell me how."

"Is this the third degree?" said Armiston.

"It looks like it," said the deputy grimly as he gnawed at his stubby mustache. Armiston drew a long breath, like one who realizes how hopeless is his situation. He began to speak in a low tone. All the while the deputy glared at Godahl's inventor with his accusing eye.

"When I was sitting in the treasure room with the Wentworths and my wife, playing auction bridge, I dismissed the puzzle of the door as easily solved by means of the brazing flame. The problem was not to get into the house or into this room, but to find the ruby. It was not in the safe."

"No, of course not. I suppose your friend on the train was kind enough to tell you that. He had probably looked there himself."

"Gad! He did tell me that, come to think of it. Well, I studied that room. I was sure the white ruby, if it really existed, was within ten feet of me. I examined the floor, the ceiling, the walls. No result. But," he said, shivering as if in a draft of cold air, "there was a chest in that room made of Lombardy oak." The harassed author buried his face in his hands. "Oh, this is terrible!" he moaned.

"Go on," said the deputy in his colorless voice.

"I can't. I tell it all in the story, Heaven help me!"

"I know you tell it all in the story," came the rasping voice of Byrnes; "but I want you to tell it to me. I want to hear it from your own lips—as Armiston, you understand, whose deviltry has just killed a man; not as your damnable Godahl."

"The chest was not solid oak," went on Armiston. "It was solid steel covered with oak to disguise it."

"How did you know that?"

"I had seen it before."

"Where?"

"In Italy fifteen years ago, in a decayed castle, back through the Soldini pass from Lugano. It was the possession of an old nobleman, a friend of a friend of mine."

"Humph!" grunted the deputy. And then: "Well, how did you know it was the same one?"

"By the inscription carved on the front. It was—but I have told all this in print already. Why need I go over it all again?"

"I want to hear it again from your own lips. Maybe there are some points you did not tell in print. Go on!"

"The inscription was 'Sanctus Dominus.' "

The deputy smiled grimly.

"Very fitting, I should say. Praise the Lord with the most diabolical engine of destruction I have ever seen."

"And then," said Armiston, "there was the owner's name—'Arno Petronii.' Queer name that."

"Yes," said the deputy dryly. "How did you hit on this as the receptacle for the white ruby?"

"If it were the same one I saw in Lugano—and I felt sure it was—it was certain death to attempt to open it—that is, for one who did not know how. Such machines were common enough in the Middle Ages. There was an obvious way to open it. It was meant to be obvious. To open it that way was inevitable death. It released tremendous springs that crushed anything within a radius of five feet. You saw that?"

"I did," said the deputy, and he shuddered as he spoke. Then, bringing his fierce face within an inch of the cowering Armiston, he said:

"You knew the secret spring by which that safe could be opened as simply as a shoebox, eh?"

Armiston nodded his head.

"But Godahl did not," he said. "Having recognized this terrible chest," went on the author, "I guessed it must be the hiding-place of the jewel—for two reasons: In the first place Mrs. Wentworth had avoided showing it to us. She passed it by as a mere bit of curious furniture. Second, it was too big to go through the door or any one of the windows. They must have gone to the trouble of taking down the wall to get that thing in there. Something of a task, too, considering it weighs about two tons."

"You didn't bring out that point in your story."

"Didn't I? I fully intended to."

"Maybe," said the deputy, watching his man sharply, "it so impressed your friend who paid your carfare to New Haven that he clipped it out of the manuscript when he borrowed it."

"There is no humor in this affair, sir, if you will pardon me," said Armiston.

"That is quite true. Go ahead."

"The rest you know. Godahl, in my story—the thief in real life—had to sacrifice a life to open that chest. So he corrupted a small kitchen servant, filling his pockets with these other jewels, and told him to touch the spring."

"You murdered that man in cold blood," said the deputy, rising and pacing the floor. "The poor deluded devil, from the looks of what's left of him, never let out a whimper, never knew what hit him. Here, take some more of this brandy. Your nerves are in a bad way."

"What I can't make out is this," said Armiston after a time. "There was a million dollars' worth of stuff in that room that could have been put into a quart measure. Why did not this thief, who was willing to go to all the trouble to get the white ruby, take some of the jewels? Nothing is missing besides the white ruby, as I understand it. Is there?"

"No," said the deputy. "Not a thing. Here comes a messenger boy."

"For Mr. Armiston? Yes," he said to the entering maid. The boy handed him a package for which the deputy signed.

"This is for you," he said, turning to Armiston as he closed the door. "Open it."

When the package was opened the first object to greet their eyes was a roll of bills.

"This grows interesting," said Byrnes. He counted the money. "Thirty-nine dollars. Your friend evidently is returning the money he stole from you at the station. What does he have to say for himself? I see there is a note."

He reached over and took the paper out of Armiston's hands. It was ordinary bond stationery, with no identifying marks of any consequence. The note was written in bronze ink, in a careful copperplate hand, very small and precise. It read:

"*Most Excellency Sir:* Herewith, most honored dollars I am dispatching complete. Regretful extremely of sad blood being not to be prevented. Accept trifle from true friend."

That was all.

"There's a jeweler's box," said Byrnes. "Open it."

Inside the box was a lozenge-shaped diamond about the size of a little fingernail. It hung from a tiny bar of silver, highly polished and devoid of ornament. On the back under the clasp-pin were several microscopic characters.

* * *

There were several obvious clues to be followed—the messenger boy, the lawyers who induced the deaf butler to go to Ireland on what later proved to be a wild-goose chase, the employment agency through which the new butler had been secured, and so on. But all of these avenues proved too respectable to yield results. Deputy Byrnes had early arrived at his own conclusions, by virtue of the knowledge he had gained as government agent, yet to appease the popular indignation he kept up a desultory search for the criminal.

It was natural that Armiston should think of his friend Johanssen at this juncture. Johanssen possessed that wonderful oriental capacity of aloofness which we Westerners are so ready to term indifference or lack of curiosity.

"No, I thank you," said Johanssen. "I'd rather not mix in."

The pleadings of the author were in vain. His words fell on deaf ears.

"If you will not lift a hand because of your friendship for me," said Armiston bitterly, "then think of the law. Surely there is something due justice, when both robbery and bloody murder have been committed!"

"Justice!" cried Johanssen in scorn. "Justice, you say! My friend, if you steal from me, and I reclaim by force that which is mine, is that injustice? If you cannot see the idea behind that, surely, then, I cannot explain it to you."

"Answer one question," said Armiston. "Have you any idea who the man was I met on the train?"

"For your own peace of mind—yes. As a clue leading to what you so glibly term justice—pshaw! To-night's sundown would be easier for you to catch than this man if I know him. Mind you, Armiston, I do not know. But I believe. Here is what I believe:

"In a dozen courts of kings and petty princelings that I know of in the East there are Westerners retained as advisers—fiscal agents they usually call them. Usually they are American or English, or occasionally German.

"Now I ask you a question. Say that you were in the hire of a heathen prince, and a grievous wrong were done that prince, say, by a thoughtless woman who had not the least conception of the beauty of an idea she had outraged. Merely for the possession of a bauble, valueless to her except to appease vanity, she ruthlessly rode down a superstition that was as holy to this prince as your own belief in Christ is to you. What would you do?"

Without waiting for Armiston to answer, Johanssen went on:

"I know a man—You say this man you met on the train had wonderful hands, did he not? Yes, I thought so. Armiston, I know a man who would not sit idly by and smile to himself over the ridiculous fuss occasioned by the loss of an imperfect stone—off color, badly cut, and everything else. Neither would he laugh at the superstition behind it. He would say to himself: 'This superstition is older by several thousand years than I or my people.' And this man, whom I know, is brave enough to right that wrong himself if his underlings failed."

"I follow," said Armiston dully.

"But," said Johanssen, leaning forward and tapping the author on the knee—"but the task proves too big for him. What did he do? He asked the cleverest man in the world to help him. And Godahl helped him. That," said Johanssen, interrupting Armiston with a raised finger, "is the story of the white ruby. The Story of the White Ruby you see, is something infinitely finer than mere vulgar robbery and murder, as the author of the Infallible Godahl conceived it."

Johanssen said a great deal more. In the end he took the lozenge-shaped diamond pendant and put the glass on the silver bar, that his friend might see the inscription on the back. He told him what the inscription signified—"Brother of a King," and, furthermore, how few men alive possessed the capacity for brotherhood.

"I think," said Armiston as he was about to take his leave, "that I will travel in the Straits this winter."

"If you do," said Johanssen, "I earnestly advise you to leave your Godahl and his decoration at home."

II
BLIND MAN'S BUFF

"Godahl, attend!" said that adept in smart crime to himself as he paused at the curb. "You think you are clever; but there goes your better."

He had to step into the street to make way for the crowd that overflowed the pavement—men and women, newsboys, even unhorsed actors leaving their pillars for the time for the passing sensation, the beginning of the homing matinee crowds—all elbowing for a place about a tall, slender man in black who, as he advanced, gently tapped a cane-point before him. What attracted the vortex, however, was not so much the man himself as the fact that he wore a black mask. The mask was impenetrable. People said he had no eyes. It was Malvino the Magician, born to eternal darkness. From a child, so the story went, his fingers had been schooled with the same cruel science they ply in Russia to educate the toes of their ballet dancers—until his fingers saw for him.

Head erect, shoulders squared, body poised with the precision of a skater—his handsome, clear-cut features, almost ghastly in contrast to the band of silk ribbon that covered the sockets where sight should have been—he advanced with military step in the cleared circle that ever revolved about him, his slender cane shooting out now and again with the flash of a rapier to tap-tap-tap on the flags. Why pay for an orchestra chair to witness his feats of legerdemain? Peopling silk hats with fecund families of rabbits, or even discovering a hogshead of boiling water in an innocent bystander's vest pocket, was as nothing to this theatric negotiation of Broadway in the rush hour of late Saturday afternoon. Malvino the Magician seemed oblivious to everything save the subtle impulses of that wand of a cane.

He stopped, suddenly alert to some immediate impression. The vague features relaxed; the teeth shone.

"Ah! Godahl, my friend!" he cried. He turned and advanced deliberately through the crowd that opened a path in front of him. Those wonderful hands reached out and touched Godahl on the arm, without hesitation as to direction.

Godahl could not repress a smile. Such a trick was worth a thousand dollars a week to the front of the house; and nobody knew better than the great Malvino the value of advertising. That was why he walked Broadway unattended twice a day.

When he spoke it was in French. "I am sickened of them all," he said, sweeping his cane in a circle to indicate the gaping crowd straining to catch his words. "See! We have at hand a public chauffeur with nothing better to do than to follow in the wake of the Great Malvino. Godahl, my friend, you are at leisure? Then we will enter."

And Godahl, playing his cards with enjoyment and admiration as well, permitted the blind man to open the door and help him— Godahl, possessing five senses—into the cab; pleased doubly, indeed, to note that the magician had managed to steal his wallet in the brief contact. "To the park!" ordered Malvino, showing his teeth to the crowd as he shut the door.

Godahl had known Malvino first in Rome. The great of the earth gravitate toward each other. No one knew how great Godahl was except himself. He knew that he had never failed. No one knew how great Malvino was except Godahl. Once he had attempted to imitate Malvino and had almost failed. The functions of the third finger of his left hand lacked the wonderful coordination possessed by the magician. Malvino knew Godahl as an entertaining cosmopolitan, of which the world possesses far too few.

"I would exercise my English," said the mask, "if you will be so good, my friend. Tell me—you know the lake shore in that city of Chicago?"

"As a book," said Godahl. "You are about to parade there—eh?"

"I am about to parade there," replied Malvino, imitating the accents of the other. "Therefore I would know it—as a book. Read it to me— slowly—page by page, my friend. I walk there shortly."

Godahl possessed, first of all, a marvelous faculty of visualizing. It was most necessary, almost as much so in fact for him in his profession as for Malvino in his—Malvino without eyes. In a matter-of-fact manner, like a mariner charting some dangerous channel, he plotted the great thoroughfare from the boulevard entrance to the

Auditorium. The other listened attentively, recording every word. He had made use of Godahl in this way before and knew the value of that man's observations. Then suddenly, impatiently:

"One moment; there is another thing—of immediate need. The Pegasus Club? We are passing it at this moment—eh? You are one of the—what is it they say?—ah, yes, the fifty little millionaires—ha-ha!—yes?"

Godahl looked out of the window. Indeed, they were passing the club now. They had been proceeding slowly, turning this way and that, halted now and again or hurried on by traffic policemen, until now they were merely a helpless unit in the faltering tide of Fifth Avenue; it was past five in the evening and all uptown New York was on the move, afoot and awheel.

It was said of Malvino that he would suffer himself to be whirled round twenty times on being set down in some remote neighborhood of a strange city, and with the aid of his cane find his way back to his hotel with the surety of a pigeon. But even that faculty did not explain how he knew they were passing a certain building, the Pegasus Club, at this moment. Unless, thought Godahl—who was better pleased to study the other's methods than to ask questions—unless the sly fox had it recorded in his strange brain-map that carriage wheels rattled over car-tracks a hundred yards below this point. Godahl smiles. It was simple after all.

"I perform for your club Tuesday night. One thousand dollars they will pay me—the monkey who sees without eyes! My friend, it is good to be a monkey, even for such as these, who—but—" He paused and laid his hand on his companion's arm. "If I could but see the color that is called blue once! They tell me it is cool. They cannot make me feel how cool it is. You will go to sea with me next summer and tell me about it—eh? Will you not, my friend? But three of these—what you call the fifty little millionaires—you will tell me why they are called that—three of these came to me in my hotel and would grasp my hand. And why not? I would grasp the hand of the devil himself if he but offered it. They are surprised. They would blindfold my poor eyes—my poor eyes, Godahl!—blindfold them again, and again offer me their hands—thinking Malvino a charlatan. Ha-ha! Again I must shake hands with them! One wears a ring, with a great greasy stone. See! I have it here with me. It is bottleglass. Yet would this barbarian wear it until I in pity took it from him."

Godahl burst into a laugh. So this was the thief! Colwell, one of the so-called fifty little millionaires who gave the Pegasus Club its savor—who exhibited their silk hats and ample bootsoles in the plate-glass windows every Sunday afternoon—had been crying over the loss of a ringstone—a garish green affair for which he had paid hugely abroad. "I am a marvelous man—eh, friend Godahl?"

"Indeed yes!" agreed the other, smiling.

"Malvino the Magician sought Godahl, his friend, this afternoon. Petroff—my manager—he walks ten steps behind me, in the crowd. He taps three times with his stick. Three steps to the right. Ha!— There is Godahl! The *canaille* applaud; even Godahl must smile. My friend, Tuesday night Petroff is too clumsy. You will be my manager; but you must be somewhere else."

"Indeed not!" cried Godahl warmly; and to himself: "What does he drive at?"

"Indeed yes!" said the blind man, laying his hand again on the other's arm. "I ask it of you. You will be in other places. If you but say yes you will take me to sea in June and tell me what is the color blue. Listen! First, Malvino will play the monkey. Then I am to be locked in a room for five minutes. At the end of five minutes, if I am gone, that which I have is mine—even to their fat wallets—fat wallets like this one of yours, which I now return intact."

Godahl accepted the return of his wallet absent-mindedly. "It is what Mr. Colwell calls a sporting proposition. See! I have it in writing. It is in addition to the one thousand dollars. That I already possess. Now these fifty little millionaires, friend Godahl—are they all like the three who come to me in my hotel? The one with the slippery stone in his ring—the stone that I have—that one had eight thousand dollars—forty thousand francs—in one wallet—in one-thousand-dollar notes. Does the American nation make new money especially for such as these? The notes were new, the imprint still crisp, like the face of my watch. Forty thousand francs in one wallet! I know, because I had the wallet as he talked. No, my friend. I have it not now. I put it back. Ha-ha! What? And there are fifty of them like that.

I am to carry away what I can find! Godahl, it is told that the very servants of the club own rows of brick houses and buy consols at correct times. But fifty little millionaires! And Malvino is to be locked in a room, alone! I have it in writing."

A passing street lamp looked in and caught Godahl in the act of blinking.

"Godahl, my friend, if you will tell me what I must know, then I will teach you what you wish to know. You wish to know many things— eh? I can tell, for I always feel your eyes when you are by. Tell me now, every inch of the way—play it is the lake front in that city of Chicago."

Godahl chuckled. He did not love the fifty little millionaires. Those marvelous fingers! Malvino was playing with them in the air now in his earnestness. They could rob a poor-box! Godahl, smiling grimly, began to draw the map his friend desired. Three steps up from the street, then the first glass door. Inside, two vestibules. Past them, on the right, the smoking-room and lounge, a log fire at each end. On the left the street parlor, great table in the center, and heavy chairs, all upholstered—none far from the walls. Between the rooms, on the left wall, the electric-switch panel. Would he play with light and darkness? It would be as well to hold the secret of this panel. On the floors, deep carpets—

"Deep carpets!" repeated the magician. "It is well I know. I do not like deep carpets. And this room, where I shall be left alone behind locked doors—"

"It would have to be the cloak-room, on the left of the main entrance," said Godahl. Yes, that would be the only available room for such a test. No other rooms off the street parlor could be locked, as there were no doors. In this cloak-room there were two doors— one on the main corridor and one on the first vestibule. There was a small window, but it was not to be thought of for one of Malvino's girth. The doors were massive, of oak; and the locks—Godahl remembered the locks well, having had need to examine them on a recent occasion—were tumblerlocks. It would be rare business to see a man, even a magician, leave the cloakroom without help. And that, too, was in the bond—this sporting proposition.

"The locks have five tumblers," laughed Godahl, more and more amused.

"'Let there be fifty!" whispered the other contemptuously. "Tell me, my observing friend—who counts the tumblers of a lock from the outside—do these doors open in or out?"

"In," said Godahl—and the long fingers closed on his wrist in a twinkling.

"In, you say?"

"In!" repeated Godahl; and he made a mental note to study the peculiar characteristics of doors that open in.

Malvino buried himself in his furs. The car sped on through the winding thoroughfares of the park, and Godahl fell to counting the revolving flashes of the gas-lamps as they rushed by.

"This is the one place in your great city where I find joy," said the blind man at length. "There are no staring crowds; I can pick my thoughts; and the pavements are glass. Outside of these walls your city is a rack that would torture me. Tell me, why is blue so cool? June will be too late for the Mediterranean. We will start before. If you will but tell me, friend Godahl, so that I can feel it, I will give you the half—No! I will not. What is money to you? Are you quite sure about the doors opening in? Yes? That is good. Godahl, if I could see I think I would be like you—looking on and laughing. Let me tell you something of doors that open in—What! We are traveling at an unlawful speed! Mistair Officaire—indeed, yes, the Great Malvino! Pity his poor eyes! Here is money falling from your hair! You are not a frugal man—so careless!"

The park policeman who had stopped them to warn them against speed stood staring at the crisp bill the blind man had plucked from his hair, as the taxicab sped forward again. Malvino directed the driver to his hotel through the speaking tube, and a few minutes later they were set down there. Godahl declined dinner with his queer friend.

"I have here your wallet once more, friend Godahl!" laughed the blind magician. "The fifty little millionaires! Ha-ha! You promise? You will not be there when I am there?"

"You have my stickpin," said Godahl. "I believe you are collecting bogus stones. That one is bogus, but it was thought to be a fine gift by a friend who is now dead."

The other, with evident disappointment, returned the pilfered stickpin. "You promise! You will not be there when I am there, my friend?"

Godahl held the blue-white hand in his own for a moment as they parted. "No; I promise you," he said; and he watched his queer friend away—Malvino erect, smiling, unfaltering in his fine stride, conscious to the last dregs of the interest he excited on all sides. He shunned the elevator and started up the broad marble stairs, his slender cane tap-tap-tapping, lighting the way for his confident tread.

Godahl dined at his club—looking on and laughing, as Malvino had said with a directness that rather startled the easy rogue into wakefulness. Godahl's career had defied innuendo; his was not an art, but a science, precise, infallible. But several times that afternoon in the somber shadows of their cab he had felt, with a strange thrill, that black impenetrable mask turn on him as though an inner vision lighted those darkened orbs.

Frankly he avoided afflicted persons in the pursuit of his trade, not because of compunctions, which troubled him not at all, but because a person lacking in any of the five senses was apt to be uncannily alert in some one of the remaining four. He was intensely a materialist, a gambler who pinned his faith to marked cards, never to superstition. He believed intuition largely a foolish fetish, except as actuated by the purely physical cravings; yet he recognized a strange clarity in the mental outlook of the afflicted that seemed unexplainable by any other means.

Malvino, too, played with marked cards. After all, magic is but the clever arrangement of properties. But why had Malvino picked him? Why had Malvino confided in him at all? There were a dozen other members of the Pegasus Club who would have served as well, so far as furnishing the business of the affair; who would have entered the game as a huge joke. To hold up the fifty little millionaires in their upholstered wallow would surely set the whole town by the ears. Something of the sort was needed to bring the ribald crew back to earth. But—thought Godahl—if the task were to be done he would much prefer to do it himself, not look on as a supernumerary.

Malvino, of course, was a thief. The only reason he did not practice his profession was that he found the business of playing the monkey paid better. Then, too, as a thief he must bury his talents ; and there is nothing so sweet to the Latin as applause. Malvino could not keep his fingers quiet. Godahl had permitted himself to be stripped in their ride through sheer enjoyment of observation. There is nothing too small to be learned and learned well. Nevertheless it had irritated him to think that this master had whispered in his ear familiarly. It smacked too much of kinship. Godahl knew no kin!

As he swept the magnificent dining-room with his eyes, however, he could not repress a chuckle of sheer delight. It would be a hundred-day jest. They all conformed pretty well to type—a type against which the finer sensibilities of Godahl revolted. In the beginning the Pegasus had been the coming together of a few kindred souls— modest, comfortable, homelike; a meeting-place of intellectual men who took their chiefest pleasure in the friction of ideas. In this way the organization had come to have a name, even among the many clubs of the city.

Godahl had adopted it as his home; and—he cynically paraphrased it—he might be without honor in his own country, but never in his own home. He had always been pleased to think that when he entered here he left the undesirable something outside, like the dust of his shoes on the doormat—not that he lacked the lust of the game or a conscious pride in that slick infallibility which had made him a prince for whom other men went poor. There are times and places for all things. And this had been home.

Until, one by one, this tribe had crept in, overturned traditions— substituted the brass of vulgar display for the gold of the fine communion they did not profess to understand, much less to practice. A newspaper wag had finally dubbed them the Club of the Fifty Little Millionaires, and the name had stuck. It happened that a handful of them had been brooded in the same coop, that of a copper king who had begun at the slagpile and ended in philanthropy. As the newcomers gained ascendency the old sect of friends gradually drifted away. The pace was too fast for them.

There was truth in what Malvino had said of the servants; and there is nothing quite so unappetizing as the contempt of those who serve one meat and drink. But Godahl, looking on and laughing, still preserved the habit of picking his meals here with discriminating taste—though now he was less particular about wiping his feet on the doormat than formerly. He even indulged in play occasionally, and while he played he listened to the talk about things worth knowing.

Tonight the talk was all Malvino—at the particular rubber where he chose to play. It was to be a rare occasion. True, they were to pay the magician roundly for the séance and had offered him, besides, a sporting proposition in the shape of a written permission to carry off all his fingers could lift, but they chose to interpret sport according to their own lights. Two centuries ago it was sport in merry England to tie a gamecock to a stump and shy brickbats at it. The game was conducted according to rules carefully worked out, and was popular with all concerned—except the gamecock. Godahl at length, getting his fill, rose in disgust and passed out. At the corner the street lamp winked at him in its knowing way; and Godahl, forgetting the gorge that had risen in him, returned the wink, smiling.

Colwell, the master of ceremonies, was venturing to a chosen few that a certain faker would be ineligible for dates on a kerosene circuit in Arkansas before the evening was over, when the telephone boy brought him a message from the Victoria. Malvino had started, and was driving to avoid the inevitable crowd that dogged his steps.

The committee was giving a last touch to its properties—a camera and flashlight apparatus arranged behind a screen—when there came the familiar tap-tap-tapping of the cane on the marble steps. If the lilt of his gait were any criterion the mask was in fine fettle.

"So"—he was whispering—"three steps up from the street—two vestibules—and deep carpets. Deep carpets are bad!"

As he passed through the first vestibule this strange, impassive figure in dead black ran his fingers along the wall. There was the door, indeed, by which he would escape.

"Malvino the Magician!" cried a flunkey in gold lace as the inner doors swung open. Colwell was there, with extended hand. The hand of the other closed on it without hesitation, holding it for a moment.

"You speak no French? No? It is—most unfortunate. I speak things— and I am most awkward in your tongue. Is there the color blue here? I would touch it before I play."

He waved his cane toward the entrance. "The corridor? It is empty— yes? It is so in the bond. Thus," he cried, his teeth glowing at the circle of faces before him—"Thus am I to take away that which is mine—is it not?"

Colwell elevated a knowing eyebrow at his companions. Colwell had not been a plumber's assistant for nothing in the days of his youth. He had plugged the keyslots with molten lead. Once closed it would require the aid of a carpenter, not a locksmith—not even a magical locksmith—to negotiate the doors of the cloakroom. Colwell did not begrudge his walletful of small change at auction bridge, but he was decidedly averse to letting it fall into the hands of this blind beggar.

They helped him out of his coat. "My cane too!" he said as he handed the cane to Colwell. It was of ebony, as thin as a baton and without ornament of any kind, save a platinum top. "It is—my faithful Achates! It is—a little brother to my poor senses. It is wonderful—" He swayed slightly and put out a hand to steady himself against Colwell. "But tonight, gentlemen, in your honor Malvino disarms himself, for the—how is it?—the fifty little millionaires—ha-ha!—who are so good as to receive me."

"Am I," he continued, "to have the honor of shaking the hands of the gentlemen? I do not know." He paused as though embarrassed, shrugged his shoulders deprecatingly; and then, smiling: "Myself, as a person, is not present if you so desire—only my talents, which you buy and pay for. Ah, I am awkward in your tongue. Sometimes, gentlemen, I am the guest—sometimes I am only the monkey, with his tricks. You understand? I thank you, sir. Saunders, of Texas Union? Ah, of the landed gentry of this great country! I am indeed pleased."

A smile went the rounds. Saunders, of Texas Union, who was shaking the hand of the mask with one hand and discreetly feeling the muscles under the black-sleeved arm with the other, had been a puddler at Homestead until his talents for ragtime rescued him from oblivion and gave him Texas Union as a pocket-piece. He brought forward Jones, of Pacific Cascade; Welton, of Tono-pah Magnet; Smithers, of Excelsior Common; Jamieson, of Alleghany Western— and so on down the line. The guest, in his naiveté, seemed under the impression that the handles to the names referred to ancestral acres. These men had been named in the daily papers so often in connection with their pet manipulations in the market that they themselves had come to accept the nomenclature, using it much as an Englishman would say Kitchener, of Khartum; or Marlborough, of Blenheim.

So the mask was passed round the room. He was well worth seeing at close range. He accepted each hand with a steely grip; concentrated the vague blackness of his mask on each face, and spoke briefly and in halting phrases. In laying aside his cane he seemed to have lost something of the poise that distinguished the great Malvino on the street or on the stage; and he leaned heavily on a shoulder here, on an arm there, as he was passed from one to another. There was a tremor of excitement in the room. A diversion had been promised; but what it was to be the honorable gentlemen of the committee had kept to themselves and their confederates. Colwell, Saunders and Mason—of Independent Guano—whispered together for a moment; and when the circle of introductions was complete the guest was led to the center of the room. He took his place at the head of the big table, exploring it nervously with his fingers while he waited for the company to be seated.

What followed was somewhat tame, and they expressed themselves to that effect occasionally behind their hands. They had seen the same thing before; a two-dollar bill gave the veriest street loafer the same privilege every afternoon and evening at the Victoria—except for a few parlor pieces the Magician reserved for private entertainments. But even the makings of these were to be had for a few pennies in any one of the numerous shops in Sixth Avenue devoted to the properties of magic. It was merely quickness of hand against slowness of eye. It is said that the persistency of vision amounts to one-hundredth of a second. These fingers found ample room to work in that slit of time. Yet the circle looked on languidly, like an audience at a championship fistfight tolerating the preliminaries.

The performer had borrowed a pack of cards bearing the unbroken seal of the club, and was playing a solitary game at whist, cards faced—a trick of Malvino's, by the way, which has never been satisfactorily explained—when suddenly the barons of Tonopah, Alleghany—and so forth—sat up with a thrill of anticipation. It was evident to all, except perhaps the performer himself, that the apex of the evening was at hand. Masons softly opened the electric-switch cabinet; Colwell and Saunders moved carelessly toward the table, taking up positions on each hand of the mask, as though for a better view of the game.

Then came blank, overwhelming darkness! There was the scuffle of feet; the snapping impact of body against body; a gasp; a half-uttered cry of pain; then:

"Confound him!" It was the voice of Colwell, breathing hard. "He's like a bull Gad!—Can't you—"

Then another voice—that of Saunders:

"Steady—I've got him? Ready?"

The unseen struggle ceased suddenly. There were several in that thrilled circle that grew sick. It seemed evident that the honorable gentlemen of the committee had overpowered the Magician, were about to strip him of his mask—to show him up as the charlatan who had too long duped a city. They wanted their money's worth. Colwell was laughing, short, sharp; he had the mask now—they could hear the silken ribbon rip as it came away.

"Now! Mason, let him have it!"

The words ended in a roar of mingled rage and pain; there came a sharp snap-snap—as of bones coming away from their sockets; and simultaneously the muffled explosion and the blinding glare of the camera flashlight. And in the one-hundredth of a second of incandescence there was indelibly imprinted on the vision of the audience the figure of the Magician holding two men at arm's length, each by the wrist, their features hideously contorted. Then dead darkness fell, in the midst of which hung the imprinted scene in silhouette against a phosphorescent pall.

Some one thought of the lights. It was the Magician himself. This curious circumstance was not noted until later. The switch clicked and the chandeliers sprang into being again. Colwell held the torn mask in his hand. Every eye, still straining for sight after the shock of the flashlight, sought the blind face of the performer. It was horribly blind now, stripped of its silk ribbon. Covering the eyesockets like plasters were great black disks larger than silver dollars. He stumbled across the room—almost fell against the table; his uncertain hand sought Colwell's arm, traveled down its length and took from the fingers the torn mask and replaced it. The master of ceremonies gazed at the cadaverous face, fascinated. The room was deathly silent. The Magician flashed his teeth in a poor attempt at a smile. His voice, when he spoke, was in whispers as crisp as leaves:

"Ah—my poor eyes! I do not sell Gentlemen, I am clumsy with your words. Let me not offend those who are my friends among you when I say I do not -sell you my private self—it is only the monkey in me you can buy."

Colwell and Saunders were making efforts to soothe their arms, which were suffering exquisitely. Several men pushed forward, ashamed, to bridge the embarrassment with their apologies to the Magician, who stared at them imperturbably with the mask. Things gradually came to rights, except for the honorable gentlemen of the committee, who took the first chance to retire with their troubles. The hands of the mask were like steel and when he wrenched the bones in their sockets he had not dealt lightly.

"We proceed," said the Magician with a deprecating wave of his hand. "The room! I am to be your prisoner. It is so written."

The few members who knew of Colwell's precautions of plugging the keyslots with lead thought wryly of the fact now. If this thing went any further the Pegasus Club would be the butt of the town!

"We will forget that," said Welton, of Tonopah Magnet, assuming leadership in a movement to make amends. "Besides," he added with a laugh, "we haven't given you a chance to go through our pockets yet. You would have to escape empty-handed."

"Your pardon!" said the mask with a grand bow. "I have already taken the opportunity."

So saying he displayed the contents of his capacious pockets. He had at least a score of wallets and several rolls of bank-notes. The room exploded in a cry of amazement. Then the truth flashed upon them. When they passed the guest from hand to hand his nimble fingers had been busy substituting wads of paper for wallets.

"The hour is late," he continued, feeling the face of his watch. "I must be gone in five minutes. The room—if you will."

Welton, of Tonopah Magnet, roaring with laughter, took the Magician—they admitted now he was at least that—and led him to the door of the cloakroom.

"One favor!" said the mask at the threshold. "My coat—my hat—my faithful cane. Ah! I thank you. I bid you good night!"

The naiveté of the words was masterly. Welton, of Tonopah Magnet, drew the door shut with a slam and the lock clicked. He faced the others and turned his trousers pockets inside out comically. He was not worrying about the safety of his cash, but he did admire the deftness of those fingers.

"I am glad to say he left my watch," he said; and he put his watch on the table. It was lacking five minutes of midnight. "What gets me," he continued, turning toward the closed door, "is how we are going to get the poor devil out without a battering ram. Colwell has most certainly earned everlasting fame by his brilliant entertainment this evening."

The keys were useless now that the spring locks had snapped on the prisoner. Some one suggested sending for the engineer; but one and all agreed that the game must be played out in common decency. They all retired to the lounging-room to give the blind beggar five minutes to find out the trick that had been played on him.

At the end of five minutes they sent for the engineer, and that grimy individual appeared, loaded down with tools; he expressed it as his reverend opinion a damned fine door was about to be turned into scrap. There was one chance—that a gasoline torch might blow the lead from the keyslot. But, no—the molten metal only completed the upsetting of the fine mechanism. There was nothing to do but to cut round the lock with a compass saw.

"Cheer up, Malvino!" said Welton through the door. "We will be with you in another minute."

Just then Godahl ran in from the street. He threw his hat and coat to an attendant.

"Ha! The devil to pay—eh?" he cried excitedly. "I just this minute heard of it; and I rushed here."

"What?" said a number of voices at once.

The usually exquisite Godahl was somewhat disheveled and his eyes were red.

"Malvino!" cried he, staring at them as though perplexed at their blandness. "Do you mean to say you don't know why he didn't show up this evening?"

"Didn't show up! What do you mean?"

"You really don't know?" cried Godahl, his eyes blazing.

"No! What? Tell us the answer!" said some one with a laugh.

"The police found him bound and gagged in a deserted cab in Central Park. They've got him in Bellevue Hospital now, raving. By Gad! if I—"

The room laughed. Even the grimy engineer boring a hole to start his compass saw looked over his shoulder and grinned at Godahl.

"Don't excite yourself, Godahl," said Welton, of Tonopah Magnet. "Somebody's been stringing you. We've got Malvino here now. Gad, I wish we didn't have him! You're just in time to help us out of a devil of a mess. That humorist Colwell has plugged the locks with lead; and we can't get the blind beggar out without sawing the door down. He's sweating blood in there now."

"In there?" cried Godahl, pushing his way through the ring round the engineer.

"In there!" repeated Welton. "The kleptomaniac has got a cool ten thousand of mine."

"No!"

"Yes!" said Welton, mimicking Godahl's tone. "You didn't know there was that much money in the world, eh?"

"Let me get this straight," said Godahl, laying a hand on the engineer's arm to stop his work. "You think you have Malvino locked in there with your wallets? I tell you Malvino hasn't been within a mile of this place tonight!"

"I lay you a thousand on it!" cried Welton.

"Tut! tut! Believe me, you are betting on the wrong card." Godahl's eyes danced.

"I lay you a thousand on it!" reiterated the Tonopah magnate. "We'll have to let Malvino hold my stake until we get him out. Gad, he went through me so clean I couldn't swear at this minute that I've got on socks!"

"You are betting on a sure thing?"

"I'm taking candy from a child," retorted Welton.

"I take you!" cried Godahl, his eyes twinkling. "Anybody else want any candy? I warn you!"

There were several. It wasn't every day in the week that they could get Godahl on the hip.

"I warn you again," said Godahl as he accepted the markers, "that Malvino is not in that room. If anybody is there, it is an imposter. You can prove it in a minute by telephoning Bellevue."

The biting saw completed its half circle about the lock; the door swung open. The room was empty!

Several volunteers ran to the rear door. Their sharp chorus of amazement started the crowd tumbling after them. The rear door was off its hinges! It stood propped against the jamb. A child could see what had happened. The prisoner, laden with the cash of the fifty little millionaires, had simply drawn the bolts of the two hinges and lifted the door out of its frame. On the floor was a wad of handbills like those the rogue had left in his dupes' pockets in place of their wallets. They read: "Malvino! He Has No Eyes! Watch His Fingers!"

The fifty little millionaires gazed at each other dumfounded, feeling their pockets the while. The infallible Godahl fell into a chair, roaring with laughter. He threw back his head, kicked out his heels, buried his hands wrist-deep in the crisp bills that lined his pockets—all in cold, hard cash! On the whole, he had never spent a more profitable evening.

As for Malvino the Magician, that charlatan could be mighty thankful that it was not he whom the honorable gentlemen of the committee had subjected to manhandling. For Malvino had the eyes of a hawk. So much Godahl had ascertained earlier in the evening when he, in the guise of a murderous cabby, was subjecting the Italian to the indignity of a gag.

III
THE NIGHT OF A THOUSAND THIEVES

Tucked away toward the apex of the island at the Battery are a few irregular city blocks over which the figure of Sleep seems to hover with a finger on her lips; the stillness that falls here when the day's work is done is sepulchral.

To the west is lower Broadway, feebly sensuous even in the small hours, a thin stream of cars and the occasional rumble of the underground still evidencing that the line of life linking two days is not yet broken. To the north is Newspaper Row, glowing with its perpetual flame of eternal wakefulness, functioning stridently at the approach of dawn when only the cock should be crowing. To the east is the river, gleaming with the arching lights of the bridges, dull with the shadows of silent looming ships and creeping barges, turning to and fro sluggishly with the tide. It is drowsing, but it does not sleep. A winch rattles; the exhaust of a straining engine breaks a blank wall of darkness; and a blinding beam of intense electric blue breaks through the dull shadows of a freight-house, to show that Labor still strains and sweats—even at the darkest hour. The heart is slow, but it still pulses. The city never sleeps—except here, in this tiny triangle.

An inverted triangle—its base the Lane, where the greatest jewelers in the world are massed; its apex the Street, the financial vortex of the nation, where fortunes change hands every minute—here, where life is at its highest tension during daylight hours, it is as silent as death now, its towering facades of marble, granite and sandstone as dull as some long-forgotten city. A footfall among the long shadows starts a hollow song of echoes; a policeman, drowsing against some grill, lets fall his club, and the rattle is like the roar of artillery. No wheel is stirring; no human being abroad, except the slouching night watchmen gossiping together in some dark arch in whispers. Within a stone's throw on each hand are riches beyond definition—beyond the power of a mint to duplicate. Here are cold vaults of gold and storehouses of jewels so rare that guardians of flesh and blood have been swept aside and intricate, unerring mechanism installed in their stead. Hidden wires, as sensitive as raw nerves creep hither and yon to every corner into honeycombs of cells incased with concrete, steel and live steam.

Officer Double-O-Four was sorrowfully executing a vamp on the tessellated pavement of the corridor of the International Life Building, interjecting syncopations with snaps of his fingers to the tune of meditation that was running through his head. It was a cruel task for a young man—to be condemned to the very silences of these ghoulish defiles. All must serve, but some must stand and wait. To stand and wait with majestic uplifted finger in the maelstrom of Thirty-fourth Street and Fifth Avenue was one thing; to haunt a graveyard that could not even boast a rabbit was quite another, and not at all in keeping with the dignity he had absorbed from his book of rules when he was presented with his shield and heard his chief depicting the glory of his calling. Occasionally a night watchman in heretical gray slunk by; but it is more simple to extract blood from a stone than companionship from one of these low-caste civilians. At this hour even the nocturnal scrubwomen had long since put on their shoes and gone home.

At the lower end of his beat, toward the river, dwelt the one human being whom Officer Double-O-Four could cultivate consistently through the six weary hours of his watch. That was Long John, the hot-dog man, whose steaming kettle of frankfurters simmered plaintively throughout the hours of the night, inviting passing sailormen or spelling night-toiling longshoremen. Stealthily the whisking feet of the policeman wiped the pavement of the corridor to the tempo of his snapping fingers, as he meditated on the sorrows of life and the lonesomeness of death.

Suddenly the resonant air of the ghoulish defiles was smitten with the Bang! Bang! of an automobile exhaust. Now an automobile in itself was as welcome a sight to our policeman as a sportive whale to a ship in the doldrums; but an automobile that came to a jarring standstill with a squealing of brakes, jammed on by no tender hand, suggested not only an event but an adventure! The quick brain of our officer noted, furthermore, from the gloom of his corridor that this car came to a stop on the left side of the street, hard against the curb.

Rule Number Twenty-six in the little blue book he carried buttoned inside his blouse stated plainly that such an offense against well-seasoned traffic rules is punishable by fine or imprisonment, or both. However, from the look of things—and particularly from the sounds that emerged from the two passengers—this automobile was enjoying rare good fortune *to* be able to come to a stop at all, regardless of the rules of the road. When the muffler of the engine suddenly blew its head off with a loud bang the car was sliding down the incline in the canon that dumps Nassau Street into the hollow that was once, in the long ago, a meandering brook flanked by a romantic cowpath, still known by the name of Maiden Lane.

Our officer brought his vamping feet to a standstill and exercised his discretion. He might vary the monotony—establish a reputation for himself, in fact—by bringing in a prisoner from this solemn spot, which slept with both eyes shut at night; but, he reflected, the misdemeanor was just round the corner from the confines of his beat, and was therefore the concern of his partner, Mulligan, who was not in sight. Also tomorrow was his day off; and he must choose and choose quickly, between going to court and going fishing. He decided in favor of the latter as the season was well advanced—late October—and weakfish would be migrating at the first opportunity. He tinctured his decision with the reflection that traffic rules are made solely for traffic, a condition that obviously did not exist at this moment; and therefore Rule Number Twenty-six would never know the difference if it were not called into use for the present emergency.

The decision was proved especially happy by what followed. Evidently his new friends were in for quite a stay—at least, it appeared they would tarry to keep him company until his relief arrived. Strange noises were emerging from the engine, even now after the pistons had come to a halt. One of the passengers dismounted with much difficulty, on account of a greatcoat. He stretched himself, yawned, and divested himself of his greatcoat, and then carefully picked out the sharply-corrugated surface of a manhole cover as the couch on which he might rest while he made astronomical observations under the car. Why a man should pick out a manhole cover, sharply corrugated, in the first place, was beyond the wit of our officer. Why the man should strike a match to examine the manhole cover, to be sure he had the right one, was another rather asinine trick. This person was at length satisfied, for he rolled over on his back and with much exertion, because of his girth, worked himself under the chassis.

Our officer, seeking companionship, softly resumed his vamp and propelled himself toward the stalled car and its horizontal mechanician. The passenger in the seat was enveloped in bearskins to his chin; his chin was shrouded with a truly Bismarckian mustache; and a pair of obsolete goggles bridged the gap between the bow of the mustache and the peak of a cap. He looked exactly like the cartoons of motorists before the days of windshields.

At sight of the sculling policeman the man in bearskins mechanically began exploring the depths of his furs and produced therefrom two cigars, one of which he handed without a word to the officer; the other he applied to the recesses of his mustache, igniting the tip with a pocket lighter, which evidently he carried palmed for such occasions. He nodded a greeting to the policeman, and watched with some curiosity as Officer Double-O-Four deftly transferred the cigar to the crown of his helmet.

"Here's another for your brother," said the man in bearskins, producing another cigar; and our policeman, not at all nonplussed by the windfall, sent this second offering to join the first.

"Breakdown?" said the policeman, by way of opening a vein of sympathy and understanding.

His words seemed for the first time to awaken the man under the engine to a consciousness of his presence; for the man below—himself enveloped in goggles—thrust out his head.

"No," said the man under the car. "Not a breakdown! We are sewer inspectors, testing manholes."

The policeman readily traced the source of this wit to the wafflelike manhole cover on which the man lay prostrate, and smiled indulgently. He could while away the remaining few minutes of his watch giving advice. In these days of foolproof motors, with needle-valves, butterfly-shutters, and tubes so placed that they can be doctored from above instead of below, the sight of a horizontal motorist was becoming rare, even in the barbershop papers.

"Nineteen-seven, Herkimer!" said the policeman to himself scornfully, taking note of the hub. Once, before he became an officer, he had begun a correspondence course in automobile engineering; and he had progressed so far that he was able to classify machines according to the cryptic designs of their hubs. That was long ago. A motorist of today who was so far put to it that he drove a Herkimer of 1907 model must be far put to it indeed!

"Don't mind my friend," said the man in bearskins, contentedly drawing at his cigar. "He has been sitting up all night with this sick car and it is getting on his nerves. Do you happen to have the correct time, officer?"

It lacked five minutes of the hour of two. This seemingly innocent fact caused quite a commotion between the two motorists, and for a moment they argued in lively fashion back and forth. The thing they agreed on was that their respective watches differed by three minutes and ten seconds of eternal time, as indicated by the policeman's timepiece. Indeed, the exactness of the hour seemed of such importance to these two—apparently hung up for the rest of the night with their sick car—that the obliging officer ran across the street to verify his faith in his own timepiece by a jeweler's chronometer, ticking away in the half-shadow of a barred window. When he returned the man in furs had submerged himself to the ears in his great collar, and only the lazily winking cigar protruding from the enveloping folds gave signs of life.

The policeman squatted on his heels and held matches in close proximity to the gasoline feed, while the man underneath sweated and swore—but did not remove his goggles. Then came the welcome clatter of a distant nightstick on the pavement, as strident as a drumbeat; and Officer Double-O-Four took his leave gracefully and made his way toward the river with light foot. His relief was calling; his day off had begun; his head was full of fish. He did not once glance round. Had he done so he might have seen the head of the man in furs emerge from its enshrouding collar and turn cautiously. The man lifted a heavy instrument—which looked like a pair of bloom-shears, but might have been an automobile jack—and set it down on the pavement beside the car. Then he waited for thirty seconds.

At the end of that time, apparently unmindful of his mechanician, he touched the button of an up-to-date starter; the engine purred softly, and the car slid away as easily as if coasting downhill instead of uphill—for the car turned into the up-grade of Maiden Lane, to Broadway, and then north. The hollow silence shut down again. The canon was deserted. Only the manhole cover now marked the spot where, five minutes before, Providence had presented Policeman Double-O-Four with two cigars against his day off on the banks.

A two-hours' wink on his cot in the dormitory would fortify our sportsman for the pleasures of the day ahead—so he reflected as he divested himself of his shoes and belt and lay down to lull himself to sleep with the problem of whether the weather would be more propitious for shrimps than bloodworms, as bait. But it was not to be!

Later in his career Officer Double-O-Four more than once used the incident of this morning to drive in his lessons to the rookies who came his way, that a patrolman of the first grade must on no account exercise his discretion! Discretion is all right for captains, or even for lieutenants, on occasions; but the little blue book states clearly what a patrolman must do under certain circumstances. Rule Number Twenty-six covers the case in point. If our policeman had done his duty as he saw it he would have jugged these two night birds and appeared in court at the break of day to witness against them for violating the rules of the road. The judge would have listened to three words—"Ten Dollars!" he would have said; and, with fair winds blowing, Policeman Double-O-Four might have caught the eight-o'clock boat and the nine-o'clock train to Huguenots and had his play with the fish in spite of himself. Traffic rules are traffic rules—even in Nassau Street at two in the morning!

The superiority of bloodworms, in spite of the price, had won the debate, when suddenly the slumbers of Officer Double-O-Four were interrupted by a crashing clamor that seemed to jar the very plaster of the room. It was followed instantly by the thumping of stockinged feet falling off the forests of cots; sharp cries and indistinct commands burst in through the door of the drill-room. A volley of musketry, which seemed to come from the street, told the sleepy senses of the usherman that the automobile reserve wagon was waiting with noisy impatience at the curb. He fell into his shoes, scooped up his belt, his club, his revolver and his helmet, and joined the rush to the front room. He was buckling on his belt as he said "Here!" to the roll-call; he was buttoning his blouse as he stumbled on the heels of the man ahead of him in the double trot to the street; he was climbing into the green wagon—that holds forty men on a pinch and takes them where they want to go at forty miles an hour if necessary—when he discovered that he had tipped his precious cigars out of his helmet.

"Cedar Street! Straight across! William to Broadway! Remember—a solid line! Not a man to pass!"

Some one was shouting to the lieutenant who swung on the footboard; and they were off round the first corner at a gait that threatened to capsize them. At William the police wagon began spilling policemen as peas rolling out of a pod. Officer Double-O-Four tumbled out at Nassau, and his feet stuck to the pavement where they struck; that was orders! Not a man was to pass. Every twenty feet stood a policeman, trying his best to gather his still-slumbering wits and to make head or tail out of the situation.

There was not the familiar sting of smoke in the air that usually accounts for such a midnight upheaval. Neither was the clang of the police-wagon, to be heard on all sides now, met by the answering wail of fire-trucks' sirens—that strange wail which in the dead of night is like nothing so much as the howl of a panther with its head buried in some mud cavern. But bells, bells, bells! Everywhere the angry clang of bells! Fast, slow, whimpering, booming—they shivered the early morning air with their insistent clamor!

"First-precinct reserves! Close order—forward! Double quick!" came the bellowing order of a megaphone from the Broadway end; and the men closed up and started forward on a run. At Broadway they were shunted 'to the north. At Maiden Lane they were dropped twenty feet apart east to William.

"Not a man to pass!" roared the megaphone; and its echoes had scarcely died away when a little police automobile sped up and came to a stop. Two men got out—one was the inspector of the district; the other was a man in civilian's clothes. He was roaring at the top of his voice:

"Hell! No! Who said the Lane? Number Three Cable has gone now! Throw this line across Fulton Street!"

And before the blown reserves could get their breath they were bellowed into double-quick again, and shot up Broadway another eighth of a mile. As they were thrown cross-town at Fulton Street they were met by the advance line of scouts from Park Row—emergency reporters panting, some of them without hats or coats in the rush of the moment of alarm.

"You can't get through!" said the lieutenant, running forward to meet them.

Instantly there was the flashing of silver stars and reporters' police cards, the sesame by which the press crowds to the front row of the thrillers that are staged every hour of the day and night in this city of five million souls.

"I don't give three whoops if you are the Angel Gabriel! You can't get through! Them's orders!" roared the lieutenant; and he reached out and caught one daring fellow by the collar and sent him spinning to the gutter.

"Here's a man through from the other end!" cried one of the angry reporters. They all turned. A young man, his ulster flapping in the wind, was running toward them.

"You can't pass!" cried the lieutenant, barring his way.

"Who says I can't? Inspector Wiegand put me through at John Street. Take your hands off me! What the devil is the matter with you mutts anyway? Every reserve south of Forty-second Street is here and you've got a line strung solid round twenty blocks! And there isn't a man among you with wit enough to know what's happened! Gad! Look at that!"

His last exclamation was caused by the sudden bursting into light of the tall towers of the International Life. One by one the floors counted themselves, as some hand threw on the current at the electric switch. Then a neighboring building began to wink light through its windows; then another, and another. The Wall Street and Maiden Lane District was opening its eyes wide in the dead of night!

The shiny pavement was flooded with reflection. The dull sky overhead caught the glare and threw it back as a luminous cloud.

In the Pearl Street converting station, the Edison superintendent sprang from his couch at the clang of a warning bell and ran to the switchboard. The needle of the dial he looked at was jumping forward a thousand amperes at a time. The lone set of converters caring for the night load south of Canal Street was as hot to the touch as a flatiron under the stress of a sudden excess of electric current. The superintendent threw in one machine after another at the giant switchboard; the needle had now touched the index of the peak of the load—the normal capacity of the electric service to be had from this station.

"Who the devil is celebrating at this hour!" he exclaimed, glancing over at the clock.

It lacked five minutes of three. He ran up a flight of iron steps to a balcony hanging on the side of the south wall and peered out of the window. The skyscraper line of the lower part of the island was like a huge heap of glittering yellow jewels—every window, to the topmost of the towers, was aglow with light.

II

At seven o'clock on that momentous October morning—which was always afterward referred to by the Edison superintendent as "The time we hit the peak of the load with a jump of four thousand amps at three A.M.!" and by Officer Double-O-Four as "The day I did not go fishing!"—at seven o'clock that morning the cordon of police was still being drawn tight across Fulton to William; down William to Pearl; down Pearl to the spot where it crosses Broadway for the second time in that street's crooked career through lower New York; and up Broadway to meet the start of the line at Fulton.

Gradually, however, the excitement focused itself at a point in Dutch Street, where the new Manufacturing Jewelers' Building stands—a stone's throw from Maiden Lane. This building is the last work in the art of safety devices as applied to fire and burglar hazard. It is absolutely unburnable, they say.

Dizzy Sunday-story specialists have attempted to compute the wealth in gold and precious stones that finds its way into this tall skyscraper—given over entirely to manufacturing jewelers—in the course of a year. A knowledge of logarithms is necessary in the calculation. Knights of the road occasionally stop on the opposite side of the street and look with longing eyes at the tall facade, every window of which seems to nod an invitation. Usually these gentlemen, if they stand too long in one spot, are tapped on the shoulder by total strangers and requested to move on—back, not forward.

The old deadline, relic of the days of a great policeman, has long since passed into history as a police institution in the Maiden Lane district. The public did not take to the idea of a squad of plain-clothes police telling a man in which direction he might walk the free streets of the city, no matter what the record of that man might be; but the association of jewelers themselves, recognizing the value of the old deadline, have always maintained it at their own expense.

At seven in the morning two squads of men—one of police and the other of the gray-coated specials—getting no response to repeated knocking of the big bronze gate that closed the corridor in the night-time, set to work with sledges and jacks and soon had the gate open. Their fears were doubled by the fact that the din occasioned by the battering did not bring the body of watchmen who guarded this building during every hour of the day and night. The building was fully illuminated like the rest, showing that some hand had manipulated the switch at the first alarm. Next they attacked the inside doors. These proved to be more easily negotiable.

On the floor in front of the elevator cage they found the captain of the night watch bound and gagged, an ugly streak of dried blood matting his hair and covering his forehead. He was released; but he was found to be in so serious a condition that it was necessary to transfer him at once to Gouverneur Hospital.

Inside an elevator the rescue party found two more of the watch, bound together back to back, all but unconscious from the choking effect of ligatures about their necks. They had been chloroformed and were still in so dazed a condition that they could throw little light on the situation. Indeed, later their sole knowledge appeared to be that they had been suddenly set on, overpowered and bound. They had seen nothing.

The captains of the two squads telephoned their chiefs at once. They had found the storm center!

Deputy Byrnes of the police was a former secret-service man, drafted into the city service because of his knowledge of crime and criminals. Captain Dunstan, of the private corporation—the burglar alarm system that was living a night of history—had been one of the Deputy's chief aides in the Government work; and he possessed, in addition to a knowledge of crime and criminals, a technical skill that had enabled him to perfect a burglar-alarm system believed by experts to be absolutely invulnerable. And now, at this moment, the vaunted mechanism was a tangle of useless wires!

Three of the main cables had been cut; and, at the moment that Officer Double-O-Four was tumbled out of bed by the riot call, the indicators on the sensitive burglar-alarm switchboard in John Street—if they were veracious—reported the astounding fact that over seventeen hundred safes were being tampered with at the same moment! Seventeen hundred strong boxes bulging with wealth were shrieking for help.

Not exactly at the same moment, however; for the cunning thief had cut the cables with intervals of one minute between—first the lead-inclosed sheaf carrying nearly five hundred pairs of wires, the sensory nerves of the rich vaults lying below Cedar Street. At the deafening persistent clang of that first alarm, the authorities, dumfounded at the extent of the catastrophe, had thrown their cordon of police about this small district, drawing it so tight, that, it seemed, no man could escape.

Then with a crash the switchboard of District Number Two went to pieces; and in another sixty seconds District Number Three added its bells to the bedlam. Then it was that the police lines were moved as far north as Fulton, and the call was sent forth for all reserves south of One Hundred and Twenty-fifth Street.

Byrnes and Dunstan, summoned from opposite quarters to the Jewelers' Building, arrived simultaneously. Grave as was the crisis, as their eyes met and they clasped hands they burst into a laugh. This outdistanced even their experience.

"Picked up anybody?" asked Dunstan. "I'll wager you haven't nabbed the man who had brains enough to touch off these seventeen hundred burglar alarms at once!"

"Oh, we've got the usual riffraff," said Byrnes—"Some bums, a couple of scrubwomen, a handful of firemen from the big buildings, and so on. It's hard on them, but it can't be helped. The only thing promising was one man who had a reporter's card, but he bluffed a lieutenant and got through the lines. Well, captain," said the deputy, turning to one of his men, "what is it? Where did they spring the trap?"

The police captain saluted and led the way to the second floor of the building. This entire floor was occupied by Ludwig Telfen.

If you are fortunate enough to possess an ornament inclosing jewels of something finer than usual water, the chances are that if you take a sharp glass and look on the reverse side you will find a little mark formed by the looping together of the capitals L and T. And you can rest assured that if Ludwig Telfen made the setting, the gems it incloses are worth far more than the gold that clasps them, no matter how exquisite the setting—no matter if Benvenuto himself made the design. Ludwig Telfen once came into prominence by his refusal to assemble a certain famous brooch of pearls that had paid one hundred thousand dollars in customs duties—on the ground that they were imitations. He of a dozen jewelers and experts was the only one to discern the fraud.

"Whew! Old Telfen, eh? That's bad as a starter!" exclaimed Byrnes under his breath. The main entrance to the suite occupied by Telfen stood open. An ugly gash in the studding showed. A new light as to the daring of this deed burst on Byrnes, used to shocks as he was.

"Rough work, that!" he said, turning to Dunstan. "What was the exact hour the first switchboard went off?"

"Two-forty-five, to the second. Hell broke loose! I was asleep upstairs. I thought the roof had caved in! Then came the second and the third—seventeen hundred and fifty-six all at once! I never expect to hear a racket like that again."

"Seventeen hundred and fifty-six chances to one!" said Byrnes; and they proceeded, examining every step of the way. Here a door was battered; there a litter of glass on the floor. With nearly eighteen hundred strong boxes within a radius of half a mile shrieking Burglars! the master thief had gone straight to the mark.

There was no mistaking the mark. It stood in the middle of a great room—the famous safe of Ludwig Telfen. The grating about it was crumpled like cloth. This safe has been described so many times in the press that it is worth only a line here. Not content with

Harveyized steel, the makers constructed an envelope of armored concrete, eighteen inches thick on all four sides.

The safe stood in the middle of the room like a four-square tomb in its cathedral crypt. Even after the wonderfully ingenious locks had been manipulated a section of the floor must be lowered before the door could be opened. That section of flooring—solid concrete—was lowered now! It lay six inches below the surrounding level. Byrnes sprang forward with a cry of amazement. He seized the pilot wheel and whirled it. The great door of the safe swung silently open like some animate thing and the darkness of the interior yawned on the tense little party. Byrnes turned with a queer gesture. The gesture said:

"It's all over!"

When the door—once started on its half-revolution—touched a certain angle an electric contact was made and the interior suddenly glowed with scores of incandescent lights. On the floor lay a crude-appearing mechanism, consisting of two unusually long carbon rods bound together, though insulated from each other, and connected with an electric transformer such as is used in welding.

On the floor, too, were scores of crumpled envelopes—all empty. Metal doors that lined the walls of the interior hung slatternly on rudely twisted hinges, disclosing metal boxes—empty. Byrnes himself—matter-of-fact, unromantic, stirred more easily by deeds than by poetic suggestion—found himself trying to decipher the symbols with which the empty envelopes were penciled. Each symbol held its story of treasures of gold and gems, men's greed, women's vanity and tears. How much was gone? How much remained? Only old Telfen himself—with shrewd, pasty mask of a face, with its high, thin nose, and lips as thin as a slit in ivory—only old Telfen himself could tell.

But the thief—what a thief! On the floor, carefully laid aside, was the ransom of a king. Rare designs in special metals; fragile baskets, woven of threads of gold as fine as silk; wreaths of stubborn platinum, worked with infinite patience and skill into little nests to receive their precious jewels; the almost medieval trappings designed for the oratory of the wife of a multimillionaire—these,

magnificent in themselves, were thrust aside, ignored as dross, for
the masterpieces the famous vault contained.

While eighteen hundred bells were shrieking—crying in terror;
while cordons of police were being thrown about, so that even a
crawling animal could not escape; while guardians of the mammoth
treasure were rushing frantically about seeking the thousand thieves
in one or the one thief in the thousand—this master rogue had with
unerring hand cracked the biggest prize in the city, and with the
coolness of a connoisseur had tested, weighed and rejected—and
taken his fill!

Then Ludwig Telfen himself came, white and terrible to behold.
Byrnes established field headquarters on the spot, and his
lieutenants were coming and going with his terse commands. He re-
enforced the lines about the desolated blocks until, in police
parlance, the four streets that held the cordon together were one
continuous circle of peg-posts. But no one realized more than Byrnes
himself the futility of such a course. He tightened the lines merely
because it was the obvious thing to do—there was one chance in a
thousand that the bird had not yet flown. Newspaper men were
assaulting the lines on all sides; but all to no purpose. There was no
juice in the turnip for them. Extras were flooding the streets; throngs
were hurrying downtown by every line of cars—surging against the
impregnable police wall by thousands. But the best they could get in
the way of information was the fact that nearly two thousand
burglar alarms had gone off at the same moment and left uncovered
the richest camp in the world—measured in terms of gold and gems.

That the reserves of the whole island had now been summoned to
hold the impregnable wall was in itself a drug that fed the popular
imagination beyond the heights of reason. A mechanical system,
fairly devilish in its ingenuity, invulnerable behind its double and
redoubled lines of defense, had been swept away by a single stroke,
as a tornado levels a plain or a flood engulfs a valley.

Bankers, brokers, merchants, jewelers, goldsmiths—the aristocracy
of wealth and trade that hives in this quarter in the daylight hours
and draws on the world for capital—rushed to the scene, frantically
importunate, hurling themselves against that stubborn line that
knew no orders except from one source—the huge, silent man, with
square jaws, square mustache and square shoes, who was sitting in
the offices of Ludwig Telfen, examining a set of powerful bloom-

shears that had been found in a manhole in Nassau Street. The blades of this set of shears had a cutting strength of thousands of pounds—a child exerting gentle pressure on the powerful lever could slice a great piece of metal in twain as if it were a sausage. The emergency crew of the protective system had discovered the spot where the cables had been rent asunder early in the excitement. With their charts showing the location of every trunk of the monster nerve system of burglar-protection, they had followed up the main cables, manhole by manhole, until they finally came to the corrugated cover on which the fat man in goggles had rested himself to get a view of the astronomical inaccuracies of the inside of his car.

The manhole was a roomy affair—it had to be to accommodate men working at the cables, which are tested regularly with the finest instruments known to science.

The expert who had cut the cables had evidently spent some time awaiting the mystic hour. A dozen cigarette butts scattered about the cement well showed that he had awaited the appointed second without impatience; and having accomplished his task he had left his set of bloom-shears behind as a clue—whatever that might be worth—and had gone to the trouble of putting the manhole cover back in its seat with some care. He had probably escaped by Broadway—that meant running a hundred yards before the first section of the police cordon could be summoned. The blades of the shears were covered with a coating of lead and copper, like a film of grease. There was a calm, cool insolence about the whole thing that got on Byrne's nerves.

A bureau of identification was established at eight o'clock for the clamoring bankers and jewelers. Every mother's son of them had to be identified before he could enter the lines; and then he entered under guard and opened his safes under guard. One by one the treasure vaults were checked off as their contents were found to be intact. As the vaults were surrendered to their owners the guard would move on to the next, and the next. It was not until noon that the inventory had been made throughout the district.

Of all the district, only the strongroom—the fabled strongroom—of Ludwig Telfen had been tapped. The genius of the night, then, had jammed the entire machinery of the Street and the Lane, roused it from its bed with shrieking clamors for the police, simply for the opportunity of attacking this one prize. The white-faced Telfen, inscrutable even in this hour, deciphered the stories of the empty envelopes one by one. It was at ten o'clock when he crumpled up and was carried away. The Bentori crucifix was gone, with its one matchless sapphire; the Dolgoda pearl; the great canary diamond— the diamond of the Saffarans family—with its creepy history; a Hindustani ruby called "The Well"; a pale blue hyacinth, on whose broad table had been carved a symbol that had baffled the greatest archeologists; and a baker's dozen of unset diamonds, carefully matched as to size and color. Not a thief merely—an artist had picked here!

The strongroom of Ludwig Telfen, as we have said, stood in the middle of the room like a tomb in a crypt, with its sheathing of concrete. It was like a monolith the size of a dozen elephants. A workman with the coldest-drawn chisel would laugh at an order to drill through the adamant in an eight-hour day. Yet a hole the size of a man's thigh penetrated the mass, leading straight and true to the very heart of the ingenious mechanism hidden within—a mechanism in itself believed to be indestructible. It was not indestructible. The same brain that had known the spot to tap the monolith, and then had devised the means of tapping it, had played with the safe as though it had been a toy instead of a thing hundreds of men of talent had made their lifework. A pellet of some explosive at the right spot had destroyed the spark of life; and, once destroyed, the mechanism of the doors, as beautiful as the inside of a watch, became merely a jumble of senseless cogs.

"Can you figure it?" asked Byrnes, inspecting the huge hole in the monolith. "It's beyond me, I must admit."

"I don't know," said Dunstan; "but I am going to find out." He connected the set of carbon rods to the electric switch panel in the corridor through the transformer. "If I figure it right," he said, "there are a thousand amperes of electricity flowing through these rods when the current is turned on. One-tenth of an ampere will kill a man under certain conditions. Look at this!"

He kicked the switch with his foot; and instantly a blue-white flame, an arc of blinding intensity, shot across the gap between the ends of the carbon rods, hissing ominously. He handled the rods with his bare hands.

"Harmless as a kitten!" he said as Byrnes cried out in dismay.

He held the hissing arc against the side of the vault. The cement seemed to shrink before it and melt. It dissolved into a fine dust that hung in the air.

"They tell us that concrete will withstand any fire. It did in San Francisco. Look at that! Concrete will stand two thousand degrees of heat; but it won't stand this heat. Byrnes," he cried, sobered, as he kicked over the switch and dropped the electric torch, "when they come this good we can't beat them! We just haven't got the brains— that's all there is to it!"

III

Cap'n Ha'penny, that blue-eyed son of Yorkshire who patrolled the waters of Raritan Bay at night to locate the universities of fish for his customers in daytime, waited long and finally impatiently at the musty Huguenots wharf that memorable morning for Policeman Double-O-Four. Finally he gave it up and went out to his lobster pots.

As for Officer Double-O-Four, he dozed away the morning on his peg-post in Fulton Street, dimly conscious that a cataclysm had occurred in his immediate neighborhood, of such proportions as to rouse that hard-sleeping locality for once in its life. On the whole it pleased him to consider that there were rabbits in this graveyard after all. Such a scurrying he had never seen before in his short period as a patrolman of the first grade. Shortly after noon the order came to break ranks, and the mystic cordon, the wonder of a gaping crowd, dissolved into thin air and was gone. Our officer purchased a copy of the Press and verified his fears that high tide was due off the Hook at eleven-thirty-three A.M.—which meant that the only promise his disrupted day off now held out for him was to take all his clothes off, go to bed and luxuriate in sleep. So he wended his way slowly to the Old Slip Station. The surroundings were beginning to take on their usual air. The rattle of trucks and the odor of fish from the Fulton Market filled the senses.

A shock awaited him! As he ascended the steps and clumped across the floor to report himself out at the desk, the fragrance of cigar smoke smote his nostrils. His captain, bleary-eyed with his unusual exertions, was leaning back in his big chair, his feet cocked on the corner of the desk; and he was pulling at a cigar, painting the atmosphere with spirals of smoke—as if he had at last found the solace he read about in books.

It was not the undignified sight of his captain, with feet higher than his head, that roused the dull mind of Policeman Double-O-Four. It was the band of the cigar! The band was a brilliant red and blue; the policeman scratched his head and churned his memory.

He was painfully extracting a swollen foot from a shoe when light broke on him. It was as clear as day now. That was his cigar! He distinctly remembered the band. A kind though not over-sociable gentleman in a stalled automobile had presented him with that cigar earlier in the morning; in fact had presented him with two of them— one for his brother. And this lowlife captain had cribbed them out of his helmet while—

Officer Double-O-Four stared vacantly at a spider constructing an engineering work on a windowpane with a skill beyond human.

He slowly pushed his suffering foot back into his shoe; and—his head traveling like a Coney Island merry-go-round—he bent over and absent-mindedly began fastening the laces. He shook himself as though in a cold draft; he bit off part of a fingernail.

"Mulligan," he said, addressing a man packing a kit on the opposite side of the room, "did I hear ye was sent down already?"

"The divil take them!" said Mulligan between his teeth. "And all because somebody tampered with a manhole on me post when I was at the other ind of the beat! What's the force coming to these days, I ask. It'll cost me tin days' pay, at least, mind ye!"

Officer Double-O-Four, somewhat dazed, passed out. At the corner of Nassau and Maiden Lane he found a crowd collected about the very manhole his friend of the night before had selected with so much care as the spot on which to lie down. A pot of wiping solder, looking blue and cool, was thoughtfully bubbling over a gasoline torch; and the manhole, now open, was filled with men in jeans— plumbers, thought our officer—like bees in a beetrap. Officer Double-O-Four, mouth open like a sucker drinking in air at the top of a weedy pool of water, listened to the man on post explain the lay of the land. Then he put his hands in his trousers pockets—in defiance of the rules and regulations—and started east. At Dutch Street he picked out the Manufacturing Jewelers' Building; and on the second floor, after considerable embarrassment, he found Deputy Byrnes. Officer Double-O-Four was not exactly a word artist—more especially he was not a word artist when on the carpet under the eye of this particular superior, who had a distressing way of looking at him.

"Herkimer—1907 model!" repeated the deputy. "Very good. Report to Farley at headquarters. I'll see you there."

Now there are a hundred thousand automobiles in the city and vicinity of New York. The horsepower, make and ownership of each is a matter of record. All that is required is infinite patience—or a superfluity of clerks among whom to divide impatience. The Herkimer of the vintage of 1907 was a limited edition that was called in shortly after being put out. A few still crept wearily about the city, as though tired of life and its attending ills.

At three o'clock that afternoon an automobile drew up to the entrance of headquarters—then in Mulberry Street. It was a Herkimer, model 1907. Two detectives—undoubtedly detectives, from their closely shaved and shiny appearance—helped out a man of middle age, somewhat gray, pasty and frightened. He was chewing on a cigar that sported a red-and-blue band.

As he got down a messenger boy on a bicycle rushed up, dropping his wheel with a clatter; and seizing the prisoner—there was no doubt he was such—by the sleeve he thrust an envelope into his hand.

"Mr. Merwin!" gasped the boy. "I have been chasing you all the way down."

Had he not been so badly upset Mr. Merwin might have been astonished. As it was he stared stupidly from the envelope to the messenger boy, and thence to the cloud of reporters the detectives were beating back. He was hurried to the office of the deputy commissioner. Byrnes wheeled in his chair.

"Merwin! Ai-yi!" ejaculated the usually collected deputy. "What the deuce are you doing in this mess?"

From the expression on Merwin's face, he himself was still struggling for an explanation why two detectives had gently but firmly insisted on his driving them to headquarters just because he happened to own a Herkimer—reconstructed—1907. Byrnes turned to the others with a nod of dismissal. Then he turned on Merwin. He could not bring himself to believe that this notorious crank, this nuisance who had made himself the bane of police administrations for the last ten years, could have a guilty knowledge of the catastrophe of the morning. Yet he shut his teeth down hard, glared at the trembling yet defiant figure before him, and cried out fiercely:

"Well! Out with it! Quick!"

There was something in the attack of Byrnes that turned the average man inside out. The effect on Merwin, the crank, was peculiar. Merwin suddenly straightened up. He crushed the envelope he held and waved his hands on high. His eyes blazed.

"I have proved it!" he cried triumphantly. "The whole town is laughing at you. Burglar protection! Bah! One—two—three! I slice your cables—yes! A child could have done it! I have exploded your system. Ha-ha!"

Byrnes sprang at him with the roar of an animal. He seized the man in his grasp and hurled him against a wall.

"You and your damned patents that have made you a pest for ten years!" he cried. "Don't start that on me! Come down to earth! Who told you to do it? Who walked through Ludwig Telfen's strongroom and took his pick of what he found there while you were chopping the cables with your infernal shears? Spit it out! Who was it? Quick!"

The infuriated deputy dropped the man and backed away from him.

"Telfen? Strongroom? Took his pick? Why, man, it was to be a joke— a jest! I am—I am a genius! I needed only this to prove that my system Telfen, did you say? He—he—"

"He! He! Yes—he! Who was he?"

The inventor, who for years had striven by every means known to insane persistence to foist his worthless electrical protective system on the city, gradually collected his senses.

Byrnes got the story of the dupe piece-meal. It seemed that Merwin had encountered an engaging young dandy on a recent week-end visit to Atlantic City. This person had seemed particularly interested in, though politely skeptical of, Merwin's pet theories as to the weakness of the protective system in vogue in the large cities. So skeptical indeed was he that their somewhat heated argument had ended in a wager—a stake of one thousand dollars—that Merwin, by the simple means he had described, could not at a given hour on a given night render the treasure vaults of the city of New York hors de combat. They had settled the hour then and there. The electrician was smiling like a child when he ended.

"I have showed them up! I have showed them up!" he cried, his insane pride getting the better of him again. "With one stroke I have proved to this great city that its fancied security is as thin as—"

"No more of that! We've something more serious on just now than rival systems. You cut the cables, you admit!"

"I did—I certainly did! That's my set of bloom-shears on your desk now. This young man was a genius. There was no other way to show you. My brother took me down to Nassau Street and we waited until the cops changed posts. Lord, I know the plan of their mains like I know the humps in my own bed! Simple! Why, as a showing-up of the egregious, asinine—" In his excitement he tore apart the envelope he was crushing in his hands. Two halves of a thousand-dollar bill dropped out. "The wager! The wager! He saw it! He's paid it!" cried Merwin.

"The thief!" cried Byrnes.

On a slip of paper with the bill was the line, typewritten:

"My compliments! You have convinced me!"

Seeking the engaging young man who had made the estimable though fanatical electrician his easy dupe in the matter of looting the Ludwig Telfen strongroom, Byrnes paid a visit to the address indicated in the inclosure. Needless to say, however, neither the name nor the description the electrician furnished was recognized by the respectable landlady who answered the bell.

So ended the incident of the Night of the Thousand Thieves, the feat taking its place among the many unsolved mysteries. There were clues, it is true, but they were too insolently obvious on the face to lead anywhere. The misguided inventor passed the remainder of his days in confinement, childishly happy at having achieved his life's ambition.

It is interesting to note, in passing, that of the rare gems so carefully selected from the Telfen strongroom that morning only one was ever traced; the story has never been verified—it is a myth. At the head of navigation on the Saguenay River rests a little chapel, built by fishermen. On the cliffs above stands the figure of a Virgin, the thank-offering of those saved from the sea. The lost Bentori crucifix is said to hang in the chapel. It is mentioned, merely as a coincidence, that the exquisite Godahl, a famous cosmopolite—the Infallible Godahl—whose true character was never known until the publication of the memoirs of this Master Rogue, was once rescued from drowning at this spot.

IV

COUNTERPOINT

Aside from the fact that one Mr. Jackson, of Cleveland, had further fattened his batting average by lifting a ball over the ridgepole of the Polo Grounds clubhouse—a stupendous feat in the dogdays—there was nothing in the morning papers to excuse the waste of ink and paper incident to the running off of an edition.

Everybody was out of town and, as usual, news had followed the crowd. The serialized comics and other faithful all-the-year-round performers were still active in their respective columns; a variety actress was having herself arrested at Asbury for wearing a one-piece bathing suit; an entire Jersey jury was being hung by its twelfth member who did not believe in capital punishment; and the crafty Japanese were realistically credited with sowing the gates of the Gatun locks with rhyolite, cordite, maximite, et cetera, so that at the psychological moment (and as a diplomatic declaration of war) a Samurai in the disguise of a barber could press a button and leave the major portion of our fleet of super-dreadnoughts stranded up to its knees in the mud of the lake.

Godahl—the Infallible Godahl—languidly pushed aside his breakfast things and ran through his morning papers. He was pleased to note that only the most enterprising of the morning papers contained the item divulging the secret of the Gatun locks being built of fulminating compounds instead of concrete as was popularly supposed, the contemporaries remaining silent on this delicate subject. Godahl tossed the paper to an adjoining table where, breakfasting late like himself, sat his friend of many capitals, Adichi Yasakawa—or Yasakawa Adichi, as you will. "I see you are up to your old tricks again, Adichi," said Godahl genially.

The little Japanese looked uncertainly from the paper to Godahl, and back again, several times. He could not quite make out, when Occidentals addressed him, whether or not they were in earnest. Most of them treated him as a joke. Adichi was not a joke. He was traveling round the world slowly—so slowly, indeed, that when he reached home again he would be very wise and very old. In Germany he made wooden toys; in France he was a banker; in England he sold silks; and in America he wrote for the press. At home Yasakawa Adichi was something we do not comprehend. Here he was trying his best to be an American, if we would only let him, which we would not.

"Ha-ha!" said Adichi, still somewhat uncertain. Godahl, whom he had known in Berlin, Paris and London, had never treated him as a monkey; but Godahl had always this habit of eying him sharply, which was fully as disconcerting.

Adichi had a tinkling little voice. Of all his features, only his square, shiny teeth expressed the mirth that his exclamation implied. He looked at Godahl several times to ascertain if that person wished to enter into a conversation; but Godahl was again immersed in a newspaper, this time an early extra of an afternoon edition which the waiter had just brought him. So Adichi resumed his task, which was the making of embroidery designs on a piece of paper—the writing of his fathers, a system of shorthand much older than the family tree of Benn Pitman himself. Adichi could handle a typewriter with any reporter; but he could think best in his own pot hooks. Now he was transcribing music from the do-re-mi-fa-sol of accepted usage into fantastic ideographs.

Godahl, who watched the curious little globetrotter in the tiny mirror made by the planes of his eyeglasses, was candidly interested, as he was in everything Adichi did.

Suddenly, however, Godahl's wandering attention was recalled to his afternoon extra. He brought himself back to the immediate cause of his being in town this torrid weather. Stock Exchange news was on the front page! At the opening of the session at ten o'clock that morning the bears had raided Little Steel, knocking the stilts from under that restless disturber of Wall Street traffic just at a moment when a board of directors thought they had everything tacked down tight and had gone to sea.

This was good news indeed! Not because it was Little Steel that was again playing all three rings of the circus, but because there was transpiring a movement in stocks of sufficient importance to break into the front page of the newspapers. Godahl had been waiting patiently for Wall Street news to break into the first page for months now.

In five minutes he was in his own runabout, a high-powered car that breathed as easily as an engine coasting down hill. He stepped down into Cedar Street ten minutes later and turned the key in his magneto switch, so that he might find the car when he returned. It was quite probable that he would be in a hurry when he returned. Next he tossed his silk cap with his gauntlets into the dust-tight compartment behind and donned a shiny silk hat. The silk hat was his badge for this occasion. He turned the corner, swinging along with the free gait which he had acquired in his earlier youth only after arduous toil with a fencing master of repute.

The curb market, sprawling over the asphalt in front of the Stock Exchange, was bubbling like drops of water on a hot griddle. Every one seemed in a hurry or else trying to out-talk some one else. The only exceptions to the turmoil were the decrepit nags attached to obsolete hansoms roped into line in the middle of the street, and the occasional coming and going of well-fed persons clad in silk hats and frock coats, who exuded an air of prosperity and respectability.

Both the exceptions—the horses munching at their nose-bags, and the silk-hat brigade—were of interest to Godahl: the horses because of the vegetating life they pursued. These creatures came to Wall Street every day and stood there as long as the exchanges were open. None of them was ever known to carry a passenger since the days of automobiles. The bucolic idea of a stockbroker invariably associates him with a hansom cab; and probably these cabs were retained to preserve local color. Some of the nags stood with crossed legs like make-believe horses one sees in summer vaudeville; some of them hitched one bony hip high in the air; others slept through the turmoil, their noses sweeping the ground. All the cabbies looked as if Phil May had drawn them years and years ago.

It was the human animal in Godahl that caused him to prize these cab horses as one of the sights of the town. It was his thieving propensities, his adventuring genius, that caused him to be interested in the silk-hat brigade. These latter were the uptown bargain hunters, who never come to Wall Street unless financial news on the first page informs them that the Street operators are either overanxious to sell or overanxious to buy. They were not gamblers in stocks; they were investors. They merely took advantage of the periodic myopia from which Wall Street suffers; and they were content with a modest hundred per centum on the dollar in the course of a twelvemonth.

Godahl entered the mahogany offices entitled in large gold letters, Sturgis, Wheelock & Company, Stocks And Bonds ; and returning the nod of an acquaintance here and there, he dropped into a remote chair, dividing his attention between the quotation board and the mob clustering like flies about the chattering ticker. Wall Street tipple was not to his liking. He was not here to play, even though the cards lay on the table face up. Nevertheless he was pleased to note that Little Steel was still falling relentlessly, and that its sister shares were following it down somewhat like a flock of kingbirds at the tail of a swooping hawk.

A second extra edition had just exploded in the street. The riot in stocks occupied the front page; money kings were rushing to the city by special train; magnates at sea were clamorously demanding monopoly of the air for the space of the precious minute. A red-ink "fudge" —last-minute news chiseled into the stereotypes just as the presses are ready to start—recorded new low levels of prices of standard industrials and railroads. Some one was being thrown overboard. Who it might be did not interest Godahl, who glanced up from a swift perusal of the paper and murmured: "This should bring him!"

The hour was striking noon when Wellington Mapes entered the board-room. He, too, was buttoned in a frock coat and wore a silk hat, in defiance of the sticky humidity.

To look at him now, with his wrinkled visage and tottering gait, one would not suspect that in his prime, not a dozen years gone, governments of the world considered it well worth the cost to tell off shrewd agents to report his smallest doings. It was said in those days that he had an organization extending into every corner of the earth; and that he carried a full line of presidents, cabinets and royal heirs, ready to be seated or dispatched at a day's notice.

That was before age had drawn his fangs. That was before he hid himself from his closest intimates, in a seclusion none could penetrate. Though he still maintained an official residence his real home was as unguessed as the riddle of the Sphinx. Only on feast-days in Wall Street did he emerge, to play with funds that came from the four winds.

This was the man that Godahl awaited—this man who had so far outlived his time that most men had forgotten him. Godahl would run the old fox to his lair to-day. That he had promised himself.

Mapes was a striking figure still at eighty-odd: tall and gaunt, with the beak of an eagle, and shaggy brows; one eye was glass, supplanting an orb that had been gouged out by a Malay kris; in his funereal attire he looked as soft and flabby as a superannuated deacon, but for all his years he was still a man of thews. His hands were enormous; the thumb of the right hand was a full half inch longer than its fellow and no thicker than a cigar. It was encircled with a cicatrix as regular as a made ring. Years ago a Mongolian bandit with an exalted idea of justice and authority had suspended the two hundred pounds of bone and sinew of Wellington Mapes by the end of that thumb.

Mapes soon concluded his business. Like a gambler playing an immutable system, he had his tallies chalked and ready for the occasion. He wrote his check with the first two fingers of the right hand, his useless thumb trailing along behind. His eyes burned an inquiring path among the faces clustering about the ticker. Only two or three of these men were sufficiently alive to externals to note the old fox and nudge each other as he passed. The old man tottered to the door and helped himself down the flight of marble steps leading to the pavement by means of the substantial brass railing. Godahl watched him covertly through the broad window screened with a fine copper mesh like watered silk. On the last step Mapes paused and looked up and down the street.

Then a miracle occurred. The old man summoned a hansom!

Either, thought Godahl paradoxically, he sought to attract attention or to avoid it. Possibly, again paradoxically, he sought to accomplish the one by means of the other.

The cabby at the head of the slovenly line rubbed his eyes and his nose; and it required the services of a friendly messenger boy to interpret the old man shaking a menacing cane. The driver yanked the chain that upset the third leg of his hansom; he chirruped to his horse and the beast came to life with a start and a shudder. The cab drew up at the curb. The old man permitted the porter in waiting to assist him to his seat and the cab drove off without spoken directions. They would be delivered en route, no doubt.

Godahl rapidly put in a small order at the desk and he blotted his check with the self-same blotter which bore the reversed facsimile of the palsied signature of Wellington Mapes. He turned it over. The inscription ran: "Forty-four thousand three hun—" Then it was lost in a maze of confusing numerals.

It was some forty-five minutes later that the head of the somnolent line of cab horses drew up at a corner in lower Seventh Avenue that might have been the back drop of a ten-twenty-and thirty-cent melodrama. The house was an old rookery of wood, tumbling into decay. A tailor's sign decorated one dusty window, and round the corner a device rusty with age related to the passer-by that, in the heyday of its prosperity, the rookery had housed a carpenter named Jones. At the apex of the building—the house formed a triangle fenced in by an intersecting street and avenue—was a gaudy barber pole, ceaselessly churning an endless screw of red and white to advertise the industry within. In front of the barber shop, trespassing on the pavement, stood an old ailanthus tree in the act of shedding the shreds of its effulgent blossoms. Under the tree were playing a group of dirty children. Against the tree was lounging a young man who might be a plumber, to judge by the kit of tools that lay at his feet and streaks of plumbago that decorated his face. Behind this soiled mask looked out the keenest eyes in all New York, those of the exquisite Godahl.

Godahl had made a quick change from his faultless walking attire to anticipate, for the second time in three months, the coming of Wellington Mapes to this down-at-heels neighborhood. On the previous occasion, when Wall Street news broke into a first-page column and lured Wellington Mapes from his retreat long enough to invest in marked-down goods in Broad Street, he had made his way, then in a taxicab, to this sequestered barber shop, with Godahl running a warm scent; but the man the master thief had followed away half an hour later proved in the end to have two good eyes in his head and perfect thumb on his right hand, though in all other respects he was Wellington Mapes to the life. Apparently on that occasion the old world-adventurer had cause to employ a double.

Mapes now alighted feebly and walked across the sidewalk to the door, which opened for him from within. It was only a brief wait.

Everything occurred as it had occurred in the former instance. The door opened again, and a white-coated barber assisted the old man who emerged to the waiting hansom. Again it was Wellington Mapes to the life, except—as the apparently drowsing plumber noted under his lashes—both eyes were busy covertly examining the street in all directions; and one glimpse he got of the right hand told Godahl that all its members were intact. Godahl smiled discreetly to himself. It was so simple, if one only used his wits.

The cab started off. As it rounded the corner a second cab—another cab of the Wall Street vintage—appeared quite accidentally from Greenwich Avenue, turning north into Seventh Avenue in the wake of the first. And shortly an automobile that had been standing at the curb opposite began to churn, and rolled off leisurely up the avenue. Godahl was not the only one interested in the movements of Wellington Mapes on this day. It was a full half hour later that a tottering figure, muffled to the eyes, emerged from the barber shop; and, as if by magic, a taxicab rolled up to the curb and was off with the old man as quick as a flash.

"I am with you this time, my fine friend!" said Godahl to himself; and when the second taxicab was halted at Twenty-third Street by the cross-town tide of traffic an exceedingly dirty plumber, with a high-powered runabout of splendid appointments, was next in line.

II

The house was old, yet it retained in its grim signs of age every touch of its pristine magnificence. It occupied a park of probably three acres overlooking the river. A bluff overhung and concealed the tracks of a railroad running beside the placid Hudson. Hemming in the place on three sides were the towering lights of encroaching apartment houses. On the river front, for blocks, the entire slope was a net of paved streets flanked by magnificent structures of terra cotta and brick. Only this sequestered square, its lawn overgrown, its shrubbery running riot and its fences falling to decay, suggested the glories of old Washington Heights in Revolutionary days, before the city had traveled north. Over the ridge on the other side of the hill were the thirteen trees Alexander Hamilton himself planted as symbols of the units of the young nation. Ten minutes' walk to the north, overlooking the Harlem River from the heights, was the historic mansion where first the British, then the Continental officers, had gathered about the mahogany and planned their scheme of battle.

The house stood foursquare in its little park. It was of three stories, surmounted by a mansard roof. A veranda clung to its river face, one end sagging under the rotting timbers laid more than a century ago.

Godahl had chosen a rear window on the first floor, after a painstaking reconnaissance of the situation. His blood tingled. It was rarely that he indulged in an adventure of breaking and entering, and then only for high stakes, as now. But tonight there was an added zest in the affair. Mapes had been a roaring lion in his day, and to tamper with him and his possessions at his zenith would have been to invite certain destruction. All this had changed now with the coming of age, and when Godahl had set forth airily on this adventure he had not anticipated entering a web. Yet two vehicles do not dog a fictitious person without reason; and Godahl, as he worked, could not help wondering if he alone had been successful in picking up the right trail. The mere fact that the crafty old man had, on at least two occasions, taken such pains to cover his tracks after an open appearance in Wall Street gave rise to a thousand speculations.

It was simple enough for a man of Godahl's talents. The French window gave easily and noiselessly. Godahl found himself in a broad room that seemed long unused. Through an open door he caught the sound of tinkling silver. Mapes was at dinner. If Godahl's information was correct the old man was attended by but one servant. That servant would now be engaged in caring for his master's wants at table; and the light-footed thief moved forward in the gloom and lifted a dusty tapestry leading to the adjoining library.

A low light was burning there and the window curtains were drawn tight. It had the familiar pleasant smell of tenancy. In one corner was a closed desk. Adjoining it was a small safe let into the wall. In the center, under a hanging gas-lamp, was a table piled with books and odds and ends. A tray with a decanter of liquor, and a half-emptied glass stood invitingly in the center. Several loose sheets of paper lay on the table, one held down by a pen, still wet. It was as he had learned. This man, with a soul seared by avarice extending over an active life of more than fifty years, had developed one queer trait of character in his declining days. This was his infatuation for music.

Mapes had picked up and reduced to occidental scoring the weird chants of some Eastern tribes he had encountered in his wanderings. There had been no principality too mean for this famous meddler to pry into its secrets. And out of his adventurous past all he now retained was the memory of these mystic chants, whose significance stretched back thousands of years. It was said that the old man toiled unceasingly setting these airs down on paper. Apparently he had been bent over his task within a few hours, for a sheet of music scores, each inscribed in a trembling hand, with fragments of impossible themes, lay on the blotter. Godahl picked up one of them and ran over the air in his head. But he was not here through interest in exotic melody. He sought something else; yet he was willing to take advantage of what seemed an old man's abstraction in a hobby, if by its means he-could accomplish his own ends.

The sound of a heavy chair scraping over a harsh floor brought Godahl to a sense of the immediate present. Softly he slipped behind a velvet hanging and waited. It would be a long wait, but the task was worthy of the pains.

Wellington Mapes entered, the servant following at his heels and turning on the lights. The room was so heavily curtained that even the brilliant glare of the chandelier could not be seen from the outside. The servant withdrew immediately, and, as he passed through the door, the old man took a key from his pocket and closed and locked it. He would be alone. Godahl's flesh tingled again. The success of his venture largely depended on the next act of Wellington Mapes. Godahl's task would not permit him to work under the protection of sleep. He must drug the old man's senses deeper than such surface somnolence as a constitution of eighty vigorous years can call upon for solace.

Mapes seated himself in his easy chair at the table, and for several moments gazed abstractedly ahead of him. Finally he roused himself and methodically lifted a brass salver from the desk and placed it carefully on the floor beside his chair. He next took up a bunch of keys that lay beside him, rested his left arm on the arm of the chair so that the keys hung over the brass salver, and let his head fall back.

It was true then! Wellington Mapes still indulged this unique habit in his old age. In his early days Wellington Mapes had reduced the science of sleep to elementals. To lose himself in sleep until the muscles of his fingers relaxed and let fall the keys in the resounding salver, insuring an instant awakening, was all the rest he required to refresh himself for hours of toil. He had learned the trick from a famous physician and thenceforward had practised it as sedulously as the great specialist himself.

The old man's breathing became more and more regular. Godahl crossed the room with padded steps, watching the keys with fascinated eyes. Suddenly the fingers relaxed and the keys fell; but the resounding crash of their contact with the resonant brass did not follow. They fell softly into the waiting hand of the intruder. Godahl straightened up with a smile and regarded the keys in his palm. The old man was his prisoner, for the moment at least, as securely as if bound by chains.

Godahl knelt softly beside the recumbent form and gently touched the loose flesh of the throat with a thumb and forefinger. With a touch as soft as running water he exerted pressure on the throbbing carotid arteries. Consciousness would not return to that numbed brain until the blood was again permitted to resume its course. It was a trick Godahl had acquired in Java, where it is frequently used. To this device of the ancient Javanese he added another, of the moderns. He took from a pocket with his free hand a band of soft rubber, and, as carelessly as if he operated on a patient under ether, he proceeded to stretch this over the gray head resting on the cushions. He brought it down to the neck, tightened it, adjusted two soft molds of rubber in the place of his pressing fingertips, and stood away, regarding the finished task with satisfaction. Now he might go about his business.

First, there was the desk. It was a chance, a small chance; but he must be thorough. The lock came with a click, and he stood up and watched and listened. He gave thanks that Wellington Mapes spent his evenings behind locked doors, free from the eyes even of trusted servants.

Inside the desk was a litter of letters and memoranda, mostly pertaining to business—business carried on by means of the cash that came from the four winds. Godahl did not seek money. A letter attracted his eye. He picked it up and carried it over to the light. His quick sense of detail told him that the flap had been steamed and carefully re-sealed. By whom? Not by Wellington Mapes surely, because the letter was torn open raggedly at the top. He examined a second and a third—all bore the same evidence that some one was tampering with the mail of this burned-out creature of many lives. Godahl, his curiosity aroused, drew forth an inclosure. It was a torn scrap of paper. Some insignificant memoranda relating to a chart of stocks—gamblers chart stocks in much the same way as the Weather Bureau charts the weather—occupied one side. Surely there was nothing in that to repay a prying person the trouble of intercepting a man's mail.

Godahl, a magician in ciphers, studied the words and the formation of the letters; but he brought his mind away from the task, satisfied that the inscription contained no hidden message. He examined the other side of the paper. At the top it bore the embossed name of Wellington Mapes. It was a sheet of paper the old man had used in his endless scoring of his weird music. There were a dozen bars of wobbly musical notes, which, as Godahl mentally ran through them, revealed a jumble of sounds without lilt or rhythm. A second inclosure he found to have been written on a similar sheet, although the whole sheet was intact and without musical inscription. So with a third and a fourth. Some contained fragments of strange chants similar to those lying on the table beside the heavily breathing Wellington Mapes. Each of the communications was signed with the initial "R." The thrifty correspondent, whoever he might be, seemed to have made use of Wellington Mapes' waste paper.

Thrusting several letters into his pockets for examination at his leisure, Godahl put the rest aside and resumed his search.

The safe bore an intricate lock; but the fingers of the rogue, schooled to recognize the silent impact of the hidden tumblers, readily conquered the combination. There was something fantastic in the boldness with which he worked, with the sleeping man at his side. From time to time he stopped to listen, but otherwise gave no sign that the situation was perilous. In the safe was a litter of odds and ends, money, papers, a drawer of foreign coins, another of rudely carved ornaments and decorations in gold, silver and hard stones— each of them probably with its tale of blood and disaster. Godahl gave them scarcely a glance. He explored every nook and crevice of the room to no avail.

Finally, with infinite caution he ran his delicate fingers through the clothing of his unconscious victim. But Mapes wore no belt. It might be about his neck then. Yes! A pouch hung on a thong under the shirt bosom. With hands that trembled ever so little, Godahl untied the string that bound the neck of the pouch. His fingers were alive as they searched the recesses. It was here!

He drew forth a roughly shaped circlet of zircon; it was large enough for a man's first finger. The characters, microscopic in size, engraved on its surface, were of a language two thousand years dead. Godahl took from his own pocket a stone of similar size and shape. To the touch the two were identical; yet even his skill had not been equal to the task of counterfeiting the inscription of the original. He placed the substitute in the pouch and replaced the pouch in the bosom of the unconscious man. The chances were, he thought, that Mapes would not discover the fraud for months, possibly never. Yet the substitute was dross; and the original, which Godahl slipped into the back of a capacious watch case, was a passé partout, a talisman, a charm, a division of kingship, the mere possession of which—in its long-forgotten day—would have enabled its bearer to pass unquestioned through the sacred places of an ancient empire. To-day it was a curio, a mere nothing, yet, to the mind of the man now treasuring it, it was worth the risks of a night not yet ended. Mapes had confiscated the strange object from the effects of a heathen prince whom he had found occasion to make away with in the course of his business. It would be just as well, considered its new owner, if the heirs or assigns of that same prince did not find the magic stone in one's keeping.

It was worth possessing, at the expense of a great deal of pains, for one who was collecting for the sake of art itself. Some day, thought Godahl, the British Museum must own it, to treasure it away among its unseen gems and symbols. Only Godahl and the British Museum were institutions to value it at its true worth—and this Wellington Mapes who carried it in a pouch on his body waking and sleeping.

Godahl settled the old man's head comfortably against the cushions, arranging his clothing and posture with great care. So far all was well. It now remained only to escape and at the same time to unlock the fettered senses of his victim.

"I am presenting you with thirty minutes of eternal time in exchange for your bauble," he said, nodding familiarly at the sleeping form. "At your age one must treasure time beyond rubies."

Smiling blithely he stepped to the tall clock opposite and turned back the hands a half-hour. Likewise he adjusted the hands of the watch of his victim. Standing beside him Godahl measured the distance to the curtain behind which he had taken refuge on entering here. It would take quick work, the type of skill he rejoiced in. With his fingers pressing the arteries whose resumed flow would bring consciousness to the numb brain he removed the rubber band. With one movement he tossed the keys into the waiting salver and leaped to his curtain. The sleeper sat up with the start of one suddenly roused. From force of habit his fingers sought the keys in the salver. For a short space he sat idle, summoning his lagging senses; then he drew his chair to the table and resumed his eternal occupation.

III

It was midnight when Godahl found the coast clear and left the house behind him. He hugged the ragged picket fence, shadowed by its wild tumble of overgrown shrubs. A person in his attire with a face well decorated with lead grease would be given short shrift if found prowling about such a place at this hour of night. He waited patiently at the gate for a full half-hour; and then suddenly he straightened up and started down the neglected avenue.

At the corner a man stepped out from the shadow of a tree, stood stock-still in front of him, and laughed.

"Well, my fine jail-bird!" said the man genially, but with a distressingly business-like air.

Godahl peered into the leering features. Even he, alert for every eventuality, was ill-prepared for the surprise the sight of the man's face gave him. Quick as a flash, however, he had flattened one eyebrow and drawn up one corner of his mouth, a trick that transformed his features. His quick wits worked fast. The night's adventures had developed a sudden and amazing illumination.

"Scott!" he exclaimed with a sneer of contempt. "You miserable incompetent! I thought we had lost you and your pack of amateurs in lower Seventh Avenue this afternoon."

Marvin Scott was known to the master-rogue as a young dandy who did his best to ape Godahl the exquisite in the clubs he frequented.

Of good family, Scott had been advanced in the diplomatic service for several years, till his taste for wild escapades had led to his dismissal. So, at least, the story ran.

The unexpected mention of his own name coming with sneering sarcasm from this soiled person in jeans carried Scott off his feet; but he quickly recovered himself. Seizing Godahl by the shoulders—a fatal move, for the next instant his wrists were in the grip of wirelike fingers—he struggled toward the light.

"Who the devil are you?" he cried, battling furiously. "I don't know you!"

"You will!" said Godahl vehemently. He had taken a long shot, and even now that he felt sure of his ground he was entirely aware that the Infallible Godahl was lost if this man recognized him on such a venture. That the house of Wellington Mapes was being watched could mean but one thing—the old fox was at his old games again. He had long held a suspicion that Marvin Scott's long journeys hither and yon about the earth were not wholly unofficial. This thing was as clear as day. The gentleman adventurer could be here in but one capacity—as a secret agent of the state department.

"You have made a pretty mess of this business!" cried Godahl. He released his hold, but he thrust out his chin so savagely that the other, nonplussed at the sudden turn affairs had taken, shrank before him. "Do you think I have nothing better to do than to devote my time to your failures? Tell me, who among you had the wit to trace Mapes here after he doubled on you? Tell me that!

"Take your hand off your gun!" Godahl commanded, pursuing his advantage—for the other, perplexed in spite of his chagrin at the way this stranger had ridden him down, made a move toward a pocket. The stranger's tone was one of authority. In his trade no man knows his brother. "Follow me!" said Godahl over his shoulder as he started off. "And remember," he said as he waited for the other to overtake him—"I am Brown. If you call me anything else in the next half-hour I will see to it that you are started to Shanghai on foot!"

In the cover of the darkness, as they proceeded, Godahl indulged in a smile. So young Marvin Scott, in the role of a diplomatic agent, had been assigned to match his wits against the wily old Mapes. The situation that had promised to be exceedingly embarrassing was turning out entirely to Godahl's liking. His man—who it was plain to see accepted him now in his character of a disgruntled superior—was following along as tamely as if he had been accustomed all his life to take orders from a plumber. They mounted the steep hill to Broadway and then crossed to Amsterdam Avenue. Godahl picked out an all-night saloon and entered the side door. The back room was deserted; and he and his companion were soon sitting down and regarding each other with very different emotions.

"I suppose," said Godahl wearily, "that if I had let you have your way you would have further distinguished yourself by picking me up and turning me over to the police as a common housebreaker, eh?"

The other said nothing. He was trying to remember where he had seen this face before. If it had not been for the smear of plumbago, as black as lampblack, running parallel to the nose, the task might have been easier.

Godahl shook his head, a queer smile playing about his lips.

"The damnable part of it," he went on in a tone of utter disgust, "is that, now that I have finished up another one of your failures, you will get the credit for it, just as you have done in the past."

Godahl took an envelope out of his pocket, one of the three pilfered from the littered desk of Wellington Mapes.

"As a piece of fine art," he said, now enjoying the situation to its utmost, "I call your attention to this. My man, did you by any chance think that you were playing with a baby when you undertook to scrutinize the mail of Wellington Mapes? A child of five could do a better job of steaming than that!"

Scott's eyes bulged at sight of the letter, which, it was true, had already passed through his hands. All his defenses were down now. He sat silently, watching the dirty and offensively authoritative person of whom he had had the bad luck to run afoul, as that individual gave his undivided attention to the inclosure of this envelope. The adventure of the night was, after all, a mere bagatelle to Godahl. Something infinitely more interesting was on hand now.

He read and reread the words of the letter. They suggested nothing but margins and rights, dividends, and Supreme Court decisions affecting Big Business. He turned the paper over and a second time a dazzling illumination stole over his senses. He had begun to discover that two and two make four.

There was a decrepit piano in the room. Godahl stepped over to it and, holding the paper with its straggling bars of music, he fingered the notes over.

"I suppose that means nothing to you, Mr. Marvin Scott?" he said. Scott shook his head; but a dull red began to burn in his cheeks. A dozen of these letters had passed through his hands, but not until this moment had he thought of attaching any significance to the crazy scores written on the back.

"No; I suppose not," said the plumber person abstractedly. "Let me have your pen."

It was then twelve-thirty. At one-thirty Godahl handed Scott a sheet on which he had written the answer to the riddle. It was a cipher after all. The crafty old Mapes had buried it in the music score.

"It is a bit clumsy," said Godahl, "but it at least has the advantage of not requiring a written key and it can be varied at will.

The key ran as follows:

a-aa f-ba k-ca p-da u-ea

b-ab g-bb 1-cb q-db v-eb

c-ac h-bc m-cc r-dc w-ec

d-ad i-bd n-cd s-dd ex-d

e-ae j-be o-ce t-de

The dazed young man took the paper from Godahl's hand. His face was flushed with an intermingling of enthusiasm and chagrin when he looked up. Godahl, the soul of indulgence, was beaming on him.

"Reduce your score to letters, c, d, e, f, g, a, b, c," he said. "The f and the g are blinds, you see," he said. "So are the sharps and flats. When you come to a chord, disregard all but the dominant note. I see I must teach you elementals."

Scott took the letter and set to work feverishly. Soon it was done.

"By gad! Wonderful!" he cried, and he read the translation :

"Flamenco and Naos complete; Perico not later than the fifteenth."

Flamenco, Naos and Perico? Godahl rummaged his brain. Those, if he remembered rightly, were the three islands on the Pacific side of the Panama Canal which the Government was fortifying with such secrecy.

"It beats all!" cried the youth, "Outside of Goethals, and the House and Senate Committee on Military Affairs—and possibly the War College—there is not another man alive supposed to know those plans. And yet old Mapes, practically dead and buried ten years ago, so far as his ability to meddle is concerned, has walked right into the middle of things with his damnable organization and snitched the plans out from under our noses!"

"I presume," said Godahl—whose mind working back through a series of pictures had suddenly found a new inspiration—"I presume, seeing you have distinguished yourself so signally on this end of the combination, that you have not the remotest idea who is working the other end?"

The enthusiasm of the other was suddenly squelched. He blurted out his complete failure.

"Do you happen to know a smooth little Jap named Adichi Yasakawa?" asked Godahl. "He is taking one hundred years to circumnavigate the globe."

"Very well!" said Scott in surprise. "The mildest little creature that ever—"

"Yes, I know. Very mild indeed!" retorted Godahl sharply. "Remember this is your affair. I am not to be known in it, not even to the Chief! Recollect that, or off goes your head at the collarbone. Scott!" he said, leaning forward, "Yasakawa is interested in music—deeply interested in music. He transcribes it into pot hooks of his own. Don't attempt to decipher his pot hooks. That would be asking too much of you. But raid his rooms after eleven in the morning and you will find just what the government of Japan thinks of Flamenco, Naos and Perico. . . . And Scott," he added, looking very dignified and solemn, "make it a point not to know me when we meet the next time. I congratulate you on the successful termination of your assignment. I have the honor of wishing you a very good morning."

V
THE FIFTH TUBE

"It will be observed," noted the pharmacopeia, "that the size of the drops of different liquids bears no relation to their density; sulphuric acid is stated by Durand to yield ninety drops to the fluid drachm, while water yields but forty-five, and oil of anise, according to Professor Procter, eighty-five. It follows, then, that the weight of the drop varies with most liquids; but few experiments on this subject have been recorded, the oldest being contained in Mohr's Pharmacopoeia Universalis of 1845. More accessible to the American and English student are the results of Bernoulli" —and so on.

Godahl—the infallible Godahl—did not have the printed page before him, but he had visualized it in one glance only a few hours before and the imprint was still fresh on his memory. Reduced to elementals, a drop of liquid varies in size from one-third to one and one-half minims. Godahl split the difference and called a drop and a minim synonymous for his purpose. Later, if he were so minded, he might arrive at precise results by means of atomic weights. He began a lightning mental calculation as he sat idly stirring his beer of Pilsen with a tiny thermometer, which the proprietor of this Hanover Square resort served with each stein of beer.

"It should be fifty-two degrees Fahrenheit, my friend," said the master of the house, who in passing saw that Godahl was seemingly intent on the thermometer. Godahl was not intent at all on the tiny thread of mercury; rather he was studying the drops of golden brown liquid rolling off the pointed end of the glass instrument. However, it was as much as one's life was worth to dispute the proper temperature of beer at this eating place, and Godahl smiled childish acquiescence and explained that he was awaiting with impatience the rise of half a degree of temperature before he indulged his thirst.

"It should be just such a color," he mused—"possibly a little more inclined to orange—and a little sirupy when stone cold." And, with his head thrown back and his eyes shut, he completed his calculation: there should be sixty-one thousand, four hundred and forty such drops to the gallon—at ten cents a drop!

"Tut, tut!" he exclaimed to himself, conscious of feeling exceedingly foolish; it was so simple, so insolently obvious, like all great inventions and discoveries once they have been uncovered.

This was one of the three tasks he had dreamed of, each worthy to be the adventure of a lifetime—three tasks he had dreamed of, as a poet dreams of a sonnet that shall some day flow from his pen with liquid cadence; as an author dreams of his masterpiece, the untold story; as an artist dreams of a picture with an atmosphere beyond the limits of known pigments.

One was the Julius Tower, where at the bottom of a well lay thirty millions in coined golden eagles, hoarded by an emperor more medieval than modern, against the time when he must resume the siege of Paris. The second was the fabled chain of the Incas, one hundred fathoms of yellow gold, beaten into links; it lies purple with age in the depths of a bottomless lake ten thousand feet in the clouds of the Peruvian Andes. And the third—it was this nectar of the gods, more potent, more precious than the rarest of collected vintages. The Julius Tower and the fabled chain were remote—the one guarded by an alien army, the other guarded by superstition—but this nectar lay within a stone's throw of where Godahl sat now studying, with the fascination of a great discovery, the tiny drops of liquid falling from the tip of the glass thermometer, each drop shaping itself into a perfect sphere under stress of the same immutable laws that govern the suns.

"*Ach!*" cried a voice of truculence behind him, and his precious mug of beer was unceremoniously snatched away from the hand of Godahl by Herr Schmalz. In his abstraction the master rogue had violated a rule of the house—the temperature of the brew had climbed to sixty. Godahl, with an amused smile, watched the testy old host adjust the temperature of a fresh mug to a nicety, and when the mug was returned to him he drank deep at the other's insistent command.

"Every man to his own religion," thought Godahl. "His is fifty-two degrees Fahrenheit; mine is gold!"

Godahl, swinging his cane with a merry lilt, picked his way up the crooked street under the Elevated to Wall Street. To the east the Street was lined with grimy warehouses; to the west it was lined with marble. To the west was the heart of gold. Godahl turned west. Every window concealed a nest of aristocratic pirates plotting and scheming for more gold. In the street the *hoi polloi* were running errands for them, enviously cognizant of the shiny silk hats and limousines of their employers. Gold bought everything the heart could desire; gold attracted everything with invisible lines of force radiating on all sides.

An express wagon was backed up to the curb and curious pedestrians were peering over each other's shoulders, attracted and held spellbound by no more rare a sight than a pyramid of rough pine boxes, each as big as a shoebox, piled on the pavement. The boxes contained gold—ingots of gold. If the guards, who stood on each side of the sweating porters carrying the boxes inside, had not looked so capable it is more than likely that many individuals in the crowd would have remembered that they had been born thieves thousands of years ago, and fought madly for the possession of this yellow stuff.

"It should obey the laws of gravity and be subject to the stress of vacuum," mused Godahl, still delighted with the obvious idea he had discovered over his beer in Hanover Square. "I think," he wandered on ruminatively—"I think I shall reduce it to its absolute atom and beat it into a frieze for the walls of my study. Sixty-one thousand drops to the gallon! It should make a frieze at least four inches wide. And why not?" he thought abruptly, as though some sprite in him had snickered at the grotesque idea. It was in this way that the dead and buried races of the Andes prized the yellow metal—not as a vulgar medium of trade and exchange, but as a symbol of kingship, a thing to be possessed only by a king. They decorated the walls of their royal palaces with bands of beaten gold. It must have been very satisfactory, thought Godahl, pursuing his whimsical idea; at least—he added as an afterthought—for the kings!

He paused at the curb and his esthetic eye sought not the boxes of gold that lay on the pavement, but the exquisite lines of the little structure of which the barred door stood open to receive the treasure. The building was no bigger than a penthouse on the roof of any of the surrounding skyscrapers; yet, with its pure lines and its stones mellowed with the wash of time, it was a polished gem in a raw setting. It stands, as any one may see, like a little Quaker lady drawing her shawl timidly about her to shut out the noise and clamor of the world crowding in on all sides. On one side rises a blank wall twenty or more stories in height; on the other, the cold gray pile of the Subtreasury stands guard as stolid and sullen as the Great Pyramid itself.

The windows were barred, so that even a bird might not enter; the door was steel-studded; the very stones seemed to cluster together as if to hide their seams from prying eyes. The cornices were ample for a flood and the tiles of the roof were as capacious as saucers. Before the days when electrolytic chemistry came to the aid of the crude agencies of earth, air, fire and water, the very smoke that emerged from the blackened chimneys was well worth gathering, to be melted down in a crucible to yield its button of gold. The whole represented the ideal of a stronghouse of a past age. It was the Assay Office of the United States that Godahl regarded.

"If," thought Godahl delightedly, as his eye caressed the picture—"if it were painted on china I am afraid, friend Godahl, you would not sleep until the plate was secure in your possession."

The hour of one was suddenly, stridently ushered in by a crash of steam riveting hammers, like the rattle of machine guns. Little apes of men, high in the air back of the little building, were driving home the last of the roof girders of a tiny chimney-like skyscraper, which in several months' time was to absorb the functions, with ultramodern methods, so long and so honorably exercised by the beautiful little house in the street—the old Assay Office.

Godahl passed on and shortly was in his lodgings. There was mellow contentment here—something he prized above all things; and he sighed to think that he would not know this comfort again for weeks. That same day, as an expert electrician named Dahlog—with a pronounced Danish accent—he presented his union card and obtained employment at sixty cents an hour. Things worth doing were worth doing well in his philosophy; and, though he hated soiled fingers and callous hands and walking delegates, he must regard the verities.

II

The spic-and-span new Assay Office of the United States is sometimes described as the House Without a Front Door. Indeed, it has no front door; but it has two back doors, and gets along very well at that. In reality it occupies two back yards, balancing itself nicely on the party line between a parcel of land fronting on Wall Street and another on Pine. The Wall Street entrance is effected through the dingy halls of the now tenant-less Assay Office of the olden time; on the Pine Street side a tall iron paling suggests to the passerby that something more precious than bricks and mortar is contained within. There is a wicket gate of ornamental iron in the fence, wide enough to admit two men abreast, or to allow the passage of the hand trucks laden with boxes of gold and silver bullion. A long wooden ramp, uncovered—a temporary structure—connects the street with a window in the second story of the new building, which for the time is serving the purpose of a door.

Some day the precious parcel of land standing between the gaunt face of the new building and the street will be occupied by a pretentious facade, and then the magnificent plant that turns out pure gold day and night at the rate of some forty million dollars a year will be lost to view entirely. Now, to the street passenger it suggests nothing of its functions—suggests less, in fact, to the imagination than the pine boxes laden with bullion, whose appearance daily is always calculated to draw a breathless audience.

The walls are sheer, without architectural embellishment of any kind; it is, in fact, nothing more than the rear of a skyscraper, some day to be given a face.

It was four o'clock in the afternoon of a June day. The upper windows of the Assay Office stood open, and through the apertures there emerged a fine sustained hum, like the note of some far-away violin. It told the passer-by that the motor generators of the electrolytic plant within were churning at their eternal task of separating gold from dross.

A party of four men were in the act of leaving the place on the Pine Street side. One was the superintendent of the plant and another the master refiner, the two men responsible for the wealth within—two men whose books were balanced each year on a set of scales that will weigh a long ton or a lead-pencil mark with equal nicety.

A third man of the party was a Canadian government official who had come down from Ottawa to inspect this latest monument to the science of electrolytic chemistry. He was not interested in the Assay

Office as a stronghouse—it had long ago passed into tradition that the Mint of the United States, with its accessories, is inviolable; and to ask whether this latest plant of its kind in the world were burglar-proof would be to laugh.

The fourth member of the party was the chief of a division of the United States Secret Service, who in passing through the city had run down to find out whether Guinea gold owed its peculiar color to a unique atomic structure or to the presence of a trace of silver. On the answer hung the fate of two rascals he had laid by the heels.

"No; you haven't the idea yet," the master refiner was saying to the Canadian official. "We superimpose a low frequency alternating current on the direct current for the purpose of shaking out the bubbles of gas that otherwise would prove very troublesome."

"It is due to a small percentage of silver," the superintendent was explaining to the secret agent; and the latter was gnawing his mustache in chagrin, for the answer meant that he had barked a 'coon up the wrong tree.

At this point an incident occurred, seemingly trivial in itself, the significance of which, however, struck the four with the force of a thunderbolt a few hours later on that momentous evening. It had to do with the secret agent's enforced moderation in the matter of tobacco. His physician had ordered him to cut his nicotine allowance down to three cigars a day; and now, in the first throes of his abstention, he was as cross as a bear with a sore toe. The whiff of an Irishman's cutty-pipe smote his nostrils as the little party passed through the gate.

Now there is something about the exotic fragrance of a well-seasoned cutty-pipe that induces in those who happen to be in its immediate neighborhood an almost supranormal desire for a puff of the weed. Whether it was the intensive quality of the tobacco itself, the ripeness of the clay cuttypipe, or the fact that the cutty-pipe is subjected to a forced draft by reason of the extreme abbreviation of its stem—whichever of these elementary causes it might have been—the psychological effect was the same.

The secret agent stared vacantly about him. A mud rat—so the brown-jeaned scavengers whose business it is to scoop mud out of catch-basins are known—was igniting a fresh charge of tobacco in the lee of his mud cart, a water-tight affair of sheet steel. The tempted one drew a cigar from his pocket and regarded it with a scowl.

"It's the vile pipe that scavenger is hitting up as though it were a blast furnace!" explained the secret agent guiltily as he bit off the end of the cigar. "This is my after-dinner pill; here goes!"

He searched his pockets for a match, forgetting that he had adopted the practice of traveling matchless to make life easier. He appealed to his three companions, but they could not scare up a match among them.

"What!" ejaculated the secret agent incredulously. "Do you mean to say there are three able-bodied men in one bunch who turn up their noses at tobacco! I have heard," he went on, with infinite sarcasm, "of isolated instances—of individuals—like our friend, Doctor Pease, for example; but three men in one spot—I am amazed!"

It was true nevertheless.

"Will you honor me with a light?" said the secret agent, stepping over to the mud rat and touching him on the shoulder, interrupting that worthy in the act of dumping a scoopful of subterranean mud into the capacious bottom of his cart. "You seem to be the only man in my class around here," he added facetiously. "We have a vice or two in common. My friends," he said, airily indicating the three beside him, "are pale angels."

The mud rat surveyed the four with an air of vague curiosity. He went through the pockets of his jeans, but his hands came away empty; so, with the free-masonry of smokers, he offered the other the live coal in his cutty-pipe for a light, which the agent accepted gracefully.

"A most remarkable mud rat!" commented the secret agent. "Did you notice that he wore rubber gloves? I shouldn't be surprised to learn that he patronized a manicure on holidays!"

As a matter of fact, this particular mud rat did not confine his patronage of manicures to holidays. He had the finest set of fingers in Greater New York.

"Also," noted the professional thief-chaser mechanically, "his horse, which is a little curbed on the nigh side, has the number 2-4-6 burned in its hoofs."

"Yours must be a very interesting life," commented the bland Canadian, who had never before had the good fortune to dally with a real secret agent.

"It has its drawbacks at times," said the other, smiling over his cigar. "A man gets into this stupid habit of noting details, until at the end of the day his head is so muddled with facts for cataloguing that he can't sleep."

An hour passed; and still Pine Street, in front of the back window that is used as a door, gave no hint of the history then in the making to mark this day in the annals of crime. At the stroke of five the tall buildings vomited forth their hives of workers. The Wall Street District empties itself swiftly at this period of the year, when there are still several hours of daylight for sports afield before dinner for the army of clerks. Fifteen minutes later only a thin stream remained of the flood that had overflowed the sidewalks.

A pushcart man, catering to messenger boys and the open-air brokers of the curb, was resting on his cart taking stock of his day's business. The mud rat who worked at his unsavory calling with the aid of rubber gloves was still industriously burrowing in the depths of the manhole; a white-suited street-sweeper, a son of sunny Italy, with his naturalization papers in his pocket, was pursuing his task to the tune of the Miserere, with an insistent accenting of the grace-note at the antepenult.

A policeman or two swung along the curb. A truck, with wheels as big as a merry-go-round, drawn by ten spans of horses, bearing a sixty-ton girder for the new Equitable Building round the corner, rolled past the scene like a Juggernaut.

One—even one with the sharp eyes of a secret agent—might have photographed the scene at this moment and still overlooked the obvious clew to the situation. The drama was in full swing. It was nearing the hour of six when the curtain came down on the big act— marked, as is usual, by the gentle tinkling of a bell.

On the seventh floor of the Assay Office a man was seen to stop his task suddenly at the sound of the bell, and to look at the switchboard standing on the west side of the room. He crossed the room hurriedly, disappearing; he reappeared at the window, staring blankly and rubbing his eyes.

Two miles away, one minute later, a liveried page, silver salver in hand, passed through the corridors and parlors of the Holland House, droning wearily:

"Mister Hamilton! Mister Hamilton!"

"They are paging you," said the open-eared secret agent to the young master refiner. "Here, boy!"

"Telephone, sir—number sixteen!" And he led the master refiner to the indicated booth.

"Yes; this is Hamilton. Who is this? Jackson, you say? It doesn't sound like your voice. What's that? Say that again. Come close to the phone, man—I can't make out what you are trying—Empty, you say?"

The young scientist looked blankly at the narrow walls of the booth that held him. Then with a peremptory note in his voice:

"Who is this? Where are you? What is this tomfoolery anyway?"

He pressed the receiver to his ear, his heart thumping.

"Empty! The tank is empty? You are—crazy—man!"

Evidently the voice at the other end of the wire had become incoherent.

"Jackson," cried Hamilton sharply, "you are lying! You are seeing things! Can you understand me?"

He waited for the answer, which did not come—only a suppressed gasp through the telephone. "Jackson!" he cried. "Listen to me! Turn round and walk to the tank; then come back and tell me what you see! . . .Boy!" he shouted through the half-open door of the booth. A dozen pages rushed for the door. "Tell Mr. Whitaker to come to me at once. He is the man with the red mustache who is sitting on the ottoman in the smoking-room."

When Whitaker, the secret agent, thrust his head in at the door he was met by Hamilton bounding out. Hamilton's face told the agent that something big was afoot, and as the other dashed out he followed. Hamilton picked up Banks, the superintendent, on the way out.

They left the Canadian gasping and alone. The nice little dinner for four that had been planned for the evening was off. The three officials were half a dozen blocks down-town in a taxicab before the Canadian guest of honor woke up to the fact that, as the whitefaced refiner had stated bluntly, something was afoot that was not his affair.

The street scene that met the eyes of the three, as they tumbled out of their cab in Pine Street and ran up the long ramp leading to the door, was much the same as when they had passed out a short time before—the same actors in different persons, that was all. It was not until three days later that the story leaked out, and crowds surrounded the block, gazing at the gaunt Assay Office as they were wont in lesser numbers to gaze at the rough pine boxes laden with gold.

While the dumpcart driver and the driver of a steel truck were disputing the right-of-way at the Nassau Street corner, a little group of dumfounded men stood about a huge porcelain tank on the seventh floor of the building. From their awed silence the tank might have been a coffin. The tank was empty!

Forty gallons of gold, held suspended in an acid solution of the consistency of good beer at just the right temperature, had evaporated into thin air—forty gallons—sixty-one thousand drops to the gallon—at ten cents a drop! Of it now there remained only a few dirty pools settling in the unevenness of the lining.

Hanging suspended like washing on the line were two parallel rows of golden shingles. On one line they were covered with canvas, black with the scum of dross; on the other, the precious metal, still wet and steaming, had formed itself into beautiful branching crystals. But the nectar—the nectar of the gods—through which the dense electric currents worked in their eternal process of purifying, selecting, rejecting—the nectar of the gods was gone!

III

The three officials looked at each other foolishly. Each in his own way, according to his lights and his training, was doing his utmost to grasp the idea that presented itself with the force of a sledgehammer blow.

According to the testimony of the switchboard, between the hours of four and six o'clock on this June afternoon, in the year of grace nineteen hundred and thirteen, forty gallons of piping-hot gold-plating solution, valued at ten cents the drop, six thousand dollars the gallon, a quarter of a million dollars the bulk, had been surreptitiously removed by a thief—undoubtedly a thief—so much was obvious—from the inviolable precincts of the New York Assay Office, adjunct to the United States Mint. Jackson, the assistant refiner on night duty, warned of the interrupted electric current by the bell on the switchboard, was the first to give the alarm.

At first blush it would seem that a ton of hay, wrapped up in one package, would be far easier loot as to bulk. Counting two grains of gold to a drop of liquor, the very weight of the stuff would have been over ten thousand troy ounces—over eight hundred pounds; and its bulk, counting seven gallons to the cubic foot, would have been nearly six cubic feet—the size of a very respectable block of granite. Yet eight hundred pounds, six cubic feet, of the stuff, a quarter of a million dollars, had unquestionably departed without leaving a trace of its path.

As has been said, the Assay Office possesses two perfectly serviceable means of exit and ingress—back doors, it is true; but still doors. The structure possesses possibly fifty windows. Whitaker raised a window and peered out. The walls were as sheer as the polished sides of an upright piano. That the intruder might have entered by a window was a childish suggestion, quickly dismissed.

The doors were at all times of day and night guarded by intricate mechanical contrivances, of which no one man knew all the secrets. In addition there were the human guards, with their army six-shooters of the peculiarly businesslike aspect that tempts one to refer to them as guns.

The three officials all tried to say something after a time; but the thing was beyond words so soon after the impact. The secret agent, trained for such occasions, was the first to collect his wits. He began examining the rifled tank. He had not gone far before he began to swear softly to himself. The tank was composed of porcelain in a steel retainer. He pointed to the two rods that ran parallel lengthwise of the empty receptacle. These two rods were covered with a saddle of yellow metal throughout their extent.

Suspended from the rods were hooks roughly cut out of the same sheet of metal. Suspended from the hooks on one rod were some fifty canvas sacks, each the size of a man's sock. They contained crude bullion, from which the plating solution extracted its pure gold. On the other rod, suspended from similar hooks, were yellow plates ten or twelve inches long, varying from one-eighth to an inch thick, covered with a fine incrustation of yellow crystals, clustering together like grains of damp sugar.

"What is all this stuff?" he asked bluntly, turning to his companions who had sprung to his side when he exclaimed: "Is it gold?"

The two men nodded assent. It was solid gold, pure gold—even to the roughly hewn hooks. The very electrical connections were of *gold*.

"What's it worth?" demanded Whitaker.

"I could tell you in a second from my books—" began the superintendent.

"Never mind your books! A million?"

The superintendent shook his head. He could not yet grasp details.

"Half a million?"

"Easily!" responded the refiner. "Yes; quite that, I should say."

Whitaker lifted one of the incrusted plates, still wet from the solution in which it had been immersed so short a time before. He swung it on his finger by means of its golden hook.

"Doesn't it strike you as a bit strange," he said, "that a thief with wit enough to make away with six hundred pounds of your precious juice should have left behind half a million dollars in raw gold, lying loose in the middle of a room?"

This was a nut that for the time being resisted cracking. The secret agent said, "Humph!" and fingered his vest pocket for the interdicted cigar, which was not there.

"In emergencies," he said absent-mindedly, "it is justifiable." He turned to Banks and added: "See that no one leaves the building until I return. The first thing to do—it's foolish, but it must be done—is to round up all your employees and bring them here. I suppose all of them knocked off for the day with a clean shower?"

Yes; all the men had passed through the changing room, emerging therefrom after a shower bath, a fresh suit of clothes and an inspection. Such is the daily routine.

Whitaker walked thoughtfully down the ramp to the street and sought out a shop where he might procure fuel for thought—cigars; long, strong and black. Then he felt better. As he turned into Pine Street from Nassau he noted a small boy, of the free tribe of street urchins, holding up one dirty foot and howling with pain.

Whitaker's methodical mind noted that the foot was of a singularly blotched appearance, as though from a burn; but he had weightier things on hand than rescuing small boys in distress. The details of the start of the investigation were soon put through when he reentered the office. Every employee of the institution was rounded up, though it was ten o'clock before the last startled porter was led protesting before the stern officials and put to the question. The trail was blank.

"It's a blessed thing we have got you with us," said Banks, who had been biting his finger-nails since the opening of the drama. "It kind of takes off the curse."

He looked at Whitaker, truly thankful that so broad a pair of shoulders was there to take the burden.

"Humph!" said Whitaker, who was studying the toes of his shoes as though they contained the answer to the riddle. "It is quite evident," he began, "that eight hundred pounds of gold, especially in a fluid state, did not get up and walk off without help. I think," he said, rising, "that before we go farther I will take lessons in electrolytic chemistry. We haven't lost much time on this case and we can afford to waste a few minutes getting at fundamentals."

They retired to the seventh floor, the floor of the yawning porcelain tank; and in a short time Whitaker was in possession of the facts. It was a simple system, when all is said and done, this system of refining gold, which had been worked out by the greatest students of the time. The secret agent was put through the elementals of the process of transmuting gold from the alloy by means of the electric current.

"Very clever indeed!" remarked Whitaker. "Also, gentlemen, let me add that it is very clever indeed to lock up gold bars downstairs in safes that cost a fortune, and leave a tankful of the stuff standing in the center of an unprotected room like this."

"But who could come seven stories up in the air and get away with stuff of this bulk?" querulously interjected Hamilton. "The thing is preposterous!"

"The preposterous thing," said Whitaker, with his drawl, "has occurred—apparently under your very noses; and, from the looks of things, the fact that the liquor was steaming hot did not interfere with the plans of the thief in the least. What is that collection of pipes?"

He indicated a nest of black-varnished iron pipes running along the outside of the tank.

"Those are the conduits to carry the electric wires," explained the master refiner.

No sooner were the words out of his mouth than he exclaimed aloud and leaped into the empty tank, running his fingers with feverish haste over the conduit outlets.

"By Gad! I have got it!" he cried, his voice a high falsetto under stress of his excitement. "Hand me a portable light—quick!"

With an electric bulb at the end of a portable cord, he inspected every inch of the tank, more especially the outlet boxes of the electric wires. Four tubes were required to carry the electric current.

There were five. The fifth was empty of wires. So cunningly concealed it lay behind an elbow-joint that only eyes sharpened by an idea born of genius could have detected it. With a cry of triumph, the refiner dashed to the door and down the stone stairs. He was at the panel of the switchboard in the converting-room, where the electric current is properly tuned for its task of assaying. There were only four conduits leading from the upper floor—the fifth had lost itself somewhere among the studdings and joists of concrete and steel.

The astonished Whitaker, finding his recently acquired knowledge insufficient to follow the leaping mind of Hamilton, finally seized that individual and cornered him.

"What is it?" he cried.

"It's as plain as the nose on a man's face!" cried Hamilton. "That fifth tube! Good Heavens! man, are you so stupid? That fifth tube could drain that tank of its last drop by siphoning it out!" He broke away, cheering. "They have taken our gold out of the tank, but they haven't got fit away from the building yet. Find out where that fifth tube runs to and there you will find our gold!"

Through the simple means of a siphon their forty gallons of precious liquor could have been removed through an aperture scarcely larger than a pinhole. The dawn was beginning to break. Whitaker's mind, clogged by its abnormal meal of technical details, was beginning to run cleanly again.

"Stop!" cried Whitaker. "I am in charge of this affair. I want you to answer my questions. In the first place," he cried, seizing the refiner by the arm and twisting his hand above his head, "what is the matter with your hands?"

Hamilton's hands, where he had been pawing about in the electrolytic tank, were stained brown, as though from cautery. They were drawn with pain, though in his excitement, up to this moment he had not noticed it.

"Cyanide of potassium!"

"Where did it come from? Quick!"

"Oh, you fool! The tank—the tank, of course. The process—I went all through it with you. The tank contained chloride of gold dissolved in cyanide of potassium!"

"Does it hurt?" inquired Whitaker, with an irritating slowness.

"Hurt! Do you think you can take a bath in red-hot acid and—Help me trace that extra tube. How the deuce do you suppose that tube ever got there?"

Instantly the picture of a small burned foot came before Whitaker—an inspiration. He held the struggling Hamilton as in a vise.

"If you will sit still three minutes," said Whitaker, his eye gleaming and a forbidden cigar cocked fiercely, "I will guarantee to lead you to the place where your precious gold is—or was; I won't promise which. Or, here—come along with me!" he said as an afterthought; and the pair started for the street on the run.

Whitaker came to a stop on the corner where he had seen the barefooted boy yelling with pain.

"What's that?" he asked, pointing to a wet spot on the pavement where a liquid had collected in the ruck about a sewer opening. Hamilton dug his hands in the dirt and sprang up with a cry. In the mud were tiny needles of an orange yellow color.

"There it is! There's our gold!" he cried ecstatically; and then, with a despairing gesture: "In the sewer!"

Whitaker was taking advantage of the refiner's desolation to quiz an interested policeman. Yes; it was a fact that a steel dumpcart and a steel derrick wagon had brushed hubs at this corner about six o'clock, and that the shock had washed as much as a bucketful of mud out of the dumpcart.

Did the policeman happen to have the names of the drivers? He did, because there had ensued quite a flow of language over the accident, but no arrests. The derrick wagon belonged to the Degnon Company; and the dumpcart was one of the wagons of the General Light and Power Company. Whitaker broke into an easy laugh.

Half an hour later the foreman of the stables of the General Company was on the carpet before the fierce cigar. Could he produce Dumpcart Number Thirty-six, to which—Whitaker blew rings about his head—was attached a horse with a slight curb on its nigh hind leg? The horse—Number 2-4-6—was driven by a man who wore rubber gloves. Thus the expert thief-catcher.

"Simple as falling off a log!" Whitaker's gesture seemed to say as he put the question to the stable boss. Then he said:

"It all goes to show that the average thief loses in the long run in the battle of wits, because he leaves some apparently inconsequential clew on his trail—some tiny clew that is as broad as a state road to a trained intelligence. If, for instance," he said, forgetting for the moment the man standing before him twirling his hat in his hands—"If, for instance, that mud rat had not played on my one weakness, by blowing the smoke from his infernal cutty into my face, the chances are that he would have given me a long chase."

"The mud rat!" exclaimed the two officials in unison.

The trained intelligence accepted their implied and wondering admiration of his powers of divination with a nod, and turned again to the stable boss.

"Now, my man!" he said, "I want Dumpcart Number Thirty-six, the man who was driving it this afternoon, and the horse here at the gate in fifteen minutes. I will send one of my men with you."

"If you can tell me where to lay hands on it, sor," said the stable boss, still rotating his hat, "I would be much obliged to you, sor. Dumpcart Thirty-six was stolen from the stables this noon, and we had just sent out a general alarm for it through the police when your man nabbed me."

At this point in the prosecution of the investigation of the looting of the Assay Office of its liquid assets the irresistible force of the trained intelligence in charge met with an immovable post. It never got much farther. The missing wagon was found—abandoned in the Newark meadows—the humane driver having provided the horse liberally with grain and hay before departing.

Curiously enough, the interior of the wagon had been coated with some acid-proof varnish. In the bottom, crystallized by the cold, was a handful of needles of gold, to show that Dumpcart Number Thirty-six was indeed the receptacle in which the thief had carted off forty gallons of gold worth ten cents a drop.

It was a simple matter to trace the mysterious pipe from the gold tank through the junction boxes of the electric system to the electrical manhole in the street. Evidences were numerous that this extra conduit had been installed by the far-thinking thief at some time during the period when the building was in process of erection. In the bottom of the manhole were found a few pints of the precious stuff that had been siphoned down through seven floors to the street by the adroit expedient of breaking open a concealed plug.

"I must confess I am not much of a scientist," said Whitaker a week later; "and before we turn the page on this subject I want to find out one thing: Admitting that our dumpcart friend got away with a quarter of a million dollars' worth of gold in the form of mud, what value would it be to him? How could he get the gold out of it?"

An indulgent smile curled Hamilton's lips.

"The process of extracting gold from mud is one of the simplest in chemistry and mechanics. And the joke is," he went on, screwing up the corners of his mouth, "that when that crafty mud rat has manufactured it into bullion again he will probably have the supreme gall of bringing it here and asking us to buy it. The devil of it is that we shall have to buy it too!"

At this remote date the Assay Office officials are still in doubt whether they have repurchased their stolen treasure. It is worth while to say in passing that the surety companies responsible for the men responsible for the treasure of the Government Assay Office are still engaged in suing each other and the various contractors responsible for fitting and inspecting the interior of the new building.

The robbery undoubtedly had been planned and the properties arranged months ahead of time; but, aside from the fact that an expert electrician named Dahlog, who had been employed on the premises at odd times—a man with a pronounced Danish accent—turned up hopelessly missing, the case has not progressed. It promises in time to become as celebrated in court annals as the antique litigation of Jarndyce versus Jarndyce.

Whitaker seldom confessed his failures; but several months later, over cigars in the library of his friend Godahl the exquisite, he related the story—unabridged—of the most remarkable bit of thievery in his experience. It was his secret hope that the acute mind of this celebrated dilettante, who had many times pointed his researches with astounding analyses, might help to the solution. Godahl laughed.

"Let us go below the surface," said Godahl. "Abolish the lure of gold and the world will be born good again. Your mud rat is the apotheosis of the pickpocket. How much better they managed the whole thing ten thousand years ago! To the remote races of the Andes gold was not a vulgar medium of trade and exchange. It was a symbol of kingship—a thing to be possessed only by kings.

"In my small way," said Godahl deprecatingly, with a wave of his fine hands, "I have erected a monument to the Incas in this room. My frieze—have you noticed it? A poor thing! Where I have used grains of gold, they used pounds. But to me it symbolizes the same poetic idea. Will you join me in a fresh cigar? Ah! I beg your pardon! One's physician is a tyrant!"

VI
AN ALL-STAR CAST

One afternoon, when he was going home from work, a young woman who appeared perfectly normal sat down beside young Grimsy in an elevated train and asked him whether he did not think people looked silly sitting still and staring at each other the way they have the habit of doing in public conveyances. The remark struck him as being the most sensible one he had heard during his six months' residence on Manhattan Island, and just as he settled down for an interesting—though somewhat unconventional—chat with this normal person, the guard brought in a policeman and pointed her out as an escaped lunatic.

This hit young Grimsy rather hard, because he had spent his six months looking for a friend who was a sociable animal like himself. He worked in a bank, where he operated a handpower adding machine and had a cage all to himself, with a door that locked on the outside and walls and ceiling of interlaced brass ribbon, to say nothing of an armored concrete floor.

There were cages on each side of him in which were locked young men like himself; but, just when he felt intimate enough with his neighbor—with no other excuse than sheer proximity—to say good morning, his neighbor would be wafted off to some remote cage and a strange face would glower at his advances through the bars.

Once he actually did address the paying teller on his right, and that person instantly moved to the far side of his den, as though there were something in the act to affect the soundness of his surety bond.

At his boarding-house young Grimsy made ineffectual attempts to engage his fellows in social discourse; but they all answered by merely growling over their food, like a dog discussing vested interests with a bone he had cornered.

Primitive man probably was interested in nothing so much as his food at mealtime; but that archaic instinct is surely no excuse for civilized creatures who make a practice of sitting down together at one table. So he began to cultivate friendships, through the public prints, of people who had the habit or the knack of being talked about. Grimsy read about society and uptown society, and doings of the Upper West Side; and he actually began to take a vicarious delight in their antics, much as the ragged urchin who plants his nose on the frosty window of a toy shop and lets the water of his mouth and his imagination run riot.

He gloried in the hobnobbery of the august imperial Wilhelm and Mr. Carnegie; he knew which of the Waterburys made the deciding goal in the polo tournament, and the color of his pony; he could trace the consanguinity of some of the first families through numberless weddings and divorces; and for three whole days he followed with the greatest concern the choosing of the House-of-Representatives gift for the White House wedding. He knew that Mr. Gary, of the Steel Trust, left Aix-les-Bains on the twentieth and would sail from Southampton seven days later; that Mrs. Bixbie's first husband was a Strange, and that her son by her second marriage resided in Paris through choice; that Memsahib was the best mare at the Piping Rock Show; that the Culver-Stones were importing a new necklace of pearls for their daughter, who was to marry Comte de Chalvray; that Buck Stringer, of the Harvard eleven, kicked with his left foot; and that the Winstons were about to reestablish themselves socially in Washington after being ostracized in Manhattan through overindulgence in the divorce court.

People at sea, people on shore, at Lenox, at Durham, at Palm Beach—it was all the same to Moberly Grimsy; he flitted over the face of the earth in patent-leather society—in the narrow confines of his hall room—every time he opened the extra of an afternoon paper or stirred gossip with his coffee and rolls. And he spiced the whole with juicy paragraphs from a society weekly which confided to him the back-stairs talk in the most shameless fashion.

So in time he came to acquire a stock of information that would have been of infinite value to a faithful old family nurse in a three-story novel or to an editor of a metropolitan newspaper. It was, after all, merely one step in acclimatizing himself to New York, assisting in the laborious process of the transmogrification of one's soul from the person of a gregarious provincial to that of an insular New Yorker. He acquired numberless bowing acquaintances in print, but none on the street. It is hard—breaking the crust—when one comes from the country.

Do not blame young Grimsy when he began looking for queer places to eat. That was inevitable. Possibly, since he was regarded as a suspected person in the sphere that was his own, he might surprise a smile or a nod among the dwellers on the fringe. He began, of course, among the logwood and red ink of the electric-lighted restaurants off Sixth Avenue, but the stuff they gave him to eat and drink made him shiver in the wind when he got outside.

One night he stumbled into a Lombardy boarding house in Ninth Street, where, for the nonce, his spark of sociability was rekindled by a Great Dane dog that rested its chin on his table and regarded him with loving eyes so long as the division of the meat was fifty-fifty.

Another night he sat in a back room lined with wine-casks and counted twenty men—every mother's son of them fat and sporting waxed mustaches—enter with mysterious offerings, which later he discovered to consist of such things as one reads of in a fashionable short story, or on the *carte du jour* at Delmonico's or Sherry's— truffles, pates, succulent squabs, aromatic sauces, open-winged artichokes, bottles half-empty—the toll of many larders; for they were all chefs about to prepare food for themselves and eat. Somehow he had never before thought of chefs having to eat; but they did now, before his very eyes, after gathering about a red-hot range in the corner and putting the old adage of too many cooks to rout by loading the air with the most tantalizing odors.

Then they converted the pool table in the center of the room into a groaning board and, with many gibberings and gesticulations, sat down with the utmost enjoyment—except when they turned to scowl at him over his cold ham and cabbage.

Down in Pearl Street a Spanish cook treated him to a dish that made him feel like a three-alarm fire; in Washington Street he stumbled across an Armenian atrocity in which sulphur was the main ingredient; but he would not have minded the food if they all had not looked so sour when he helped himself to an empty chair and drew up to their table. Aside from the big dog in Ninth Street, not a soul in all his wanderings so much as nudged his elbow in a spirit of companionship. Even that dog had proved fickle when a roast came to another table.

On the evening of the fourth of December, young Mr. Grimsy, pursuing his avocation of seeking out queer places to eat, found himself—for the first time since he had come to the city six months before—lost.

He had left his cage at four that afternoon; and, profiting by the few hours of grace granted him by an early start, he had undertaken to explore that part of the city contiguous to the old Gansevoort Market. There were items of interest on every hand to claim his attention and befuddle his sense of direction. For instance, all the merchants—prosperous-looking persons above their collars—were attired in a common garb, a smock of white cotton that fitted them from head to heels like a priest's cassock.

On all the streets were superimposed wooden awnings to the very edge of the pavements, and from the eaves hung quarters of beef, spring lamb—clipped like French poodle dogs—pheasants, turtles, and such. A freight-car, ghostily propelled by some unseen force round a corner, gently pushed him off its track; a one-horse wagon, laden with provisions disguised by gunnysacks, disputed his right-of-way in an alley and left him in the gutter.

And at length he came on an object of unusual interest in the shape of two white-coated men, who seemed to be doing their best to teach cratefuls of live poultry not to stick their heads out between the slats when a second crate of live poultry was descending on them from a six-foot height. The poultry did not seem to mind it in the least; and it was evidently not a game, because the two strong men were very sober at their task—except when one of them found a warm egg, which frequently happened. The finder of the warm egg invariably transferred it to his pocket, indicating the score by holding up his fingers.

So interested was young Grimsy, indeed, at first in the ducking heads of the poultry and then in the egg score, that he found a comfortable wall to lean against and lighted a cigarette. It came on toward six o'clock, and when he again recalled himself to his surroundings he was astonished to note that the strings of beef and other provender, which had so gayly festooned the eaves but a brief time before, had mysteriously disappeared, and only blank boarded windows greeted him now in place of the busy shops.

He bestirred himself and started off, but to his surprise he found himself in the middle of a miniature walled city with columns and bastions and watch-towers.

Also, as he read the names of the streets, they were strange to him—such as Grace, Loew, Grant and Strong. He caught a glimpse of the river through a gate; and, deciding that it was the Hudson and indicated the west of the compass, which he had lost, he turned his back on it and crossed the now almost deserted walled inclosure to a gate at the opposite side. He struck out on a street lined with warehouses and tenements in the general direction of what he believed to be the New York that he knew. As he crossed a little square he was reminded of the object of his exploration of this locality by a sign on a dusty window which read, in tarnished and fly-bitten letters: Grittin's Dining-Room.

It had the outer appearance of a cheap coffee house. Through the dusty glass panel of the door he made out two tables, guiltless of cloth and decorated with crockery of the armor-plate variety to be found in the poorer class of restaurants. It is quite probable that Grimsy would have passed by Grittin's Dining-Room had it not been for a picture in the window. It was a crayon portrait incased in a massive gilt frame shrouded in dust. The picture bore the legend: Edward Askew Sothern, 1858.

Even then it is quite probable he would not have tarried to question himself as to the veracity of the legend—never having considered it plausible that an eminent comedian of to-day might have sprung from a stock immortal enough to be perpetuated in crayon so far back as fifty-eight—had it not been for a playbill draped carelessly over one corner of the ornate though somewhat weatherbeaten frame.

"To-night," announced the musty yellow poster, which was fully three feet long, "to-night will positively witness the first appearance on the boards of an American stage of the celebrated Mr. Wainbadge Maugham, fresh from one hundred nights of distinguished approbation at Drury Lane, in his celebrated drama entitled The Hidden Fortune; or, Every Hand Against Her. Mr. Maugham will appear in his world-famous delineation of the character of Willoughby Southerly—a gentleman detective—supported by the original cast, including Janice Mabon as Istheba—wistful and winning; Mr. Jack Gallant as Sir Everly Turncoat—a serpent ; Mr.

117

Halsey Jaimes as Honest John Wexford—bound on a parlous errand; Mr. Horace as Isaacs—a true friend; Miss Voorhes as the maid—a vixen; and numerous others; including every attention to the important accessories of atmosphere, scenery and costumes. Tickets within, or at the box office, American Theater, Bowery."

Grimsy softly opened the door and stepped inside. The place smelled musty, as well it might; the two tables—there were only two—were covered with an unsavory veneer of their calling; and against the side wall, and four feet deep at the least calculation, was stacked a heap of rusty old frames inclosing woodcuts, crayons and engravings of a type of art and free drawing long since dead. Packed round and about these, as excelsior is packed about fine china for shipment, were wads of venerable handbills.

One wad of perhaps fifty bills celebrated the return of Forrest as Jack Cade; another announced Mathilda Huron in her great character Camille—from the date, 1854, it seemed that *La Dame aux Camelias* had begun weeping some time before the Civil War. Herne the Humbug was on the eve of its premiere on another bill; and Teddy the Tiler and the Ice Witch or the' Frozen Hand were in the midst of a revival. Of historical importance was the dramatization of the celebrated pictures of Wilkes' Distraining for Rent, under the title of Rent Day, with Mr. Heywood and Mr. Hamlin in the principal roles.

Grimsy, convinced, sat down at a table, first taking the precaution to polish its surface with an old newspaper that covered a hole in the cane seat of a chair. He waited for several minutes for the appearance of some sign of ownership or at least of life; and when nothing developed he seized a spoon from a pressed-glass container and rapped it vigorously against the harveyized side of the sugarbowl, which, however, gave out only a dull thudding noise. Grimsy rose impatiently and opened a door leading to a side entry. This entry was, in fact, a long tunnel of brick leading to the street over a roughly paved floor at one end, and into blank impenetrable darkness at the other.

In the old days, when Greenwich Village was two miles from Manhattan, it was the custom of the carters who occupied this quarter to leave their carts outside at close of day and lead their tired horses to the stables in the back yard, through tunnels running between the houses. This fact Grimsy had gleaned out of a book long ago. If the book were veracious the impenetrable darkness at the far end of the tunnel must lead to a stable—probably now used as a kitchen for Grittin's Dining Room. He determined to ascertain whether this was indeed the fact; and to this end he stepped into the tunnel and picked his way over the moist, slippery stones.

The passage led for perhaps forty feet into the heart of the darkness, and abruptly turned at right angles, terminating six feet farther on in a door, through the soiled panes of which showed a dull light. Young Grimsy, in his search for something besides food with his meals during the last six months, had acquired the inevitable snooping curiosity of such an adventurer. The fact that a score of young Turks desired to set up an obscure restaurant where they might dine in peace and quiet was no reason—to him—why he should not walk boldly in and take a vacant chair, and force them to talk in whispers if they wished to continue their family confidences undisturbed; and the fact that this Mr. Grittin, whoever he may have been, advertised a dining-room on his front windows and forced volunteer customers to locate the source of food for themselves was sufficient excuse for our explorer boldly to open the door before him and step through the aperture. He did so.

Grimsy found himself in the middle of a paved yard lighted only by the pale reflection from the sky of a late winter afternoon; dark on four sides—with the exception of a far corner where two windows glowed warmly. The sound of smothered voices and the occasional clinking of tableware issuing from this corner, he turned his steps confidently in that direction, positive at last that he had stumbled on a queer place to eat and hopeful that here he might find some kindred soul to discuss topics of the day—possibly the art of acting—over his meal.

There was a fanlight in the door at the corner, but it was so obscured by grime that he did not notice it until his hand was on the knob and he was peering through the opening. He paused in the act of turning the knob.

Inside, before his eyes, was a long room evidently comprising the entire ground floor of a rear tenement, for on the opposite side of the apartment windows looked out into another courtyard like that in which he stood.

There were twenty persons in the room, mostly men; but, as he looked, there came a rattle of chairs on the floor by the near wall—at some spot beyond his range of vision—and in another second he saw three women advancing across the open floor to the far corner, where sat the broad squat figure of an old man with a magnificent head on his shoulders.

At this moment, however, the women attracted the attention of the peeping Grimsy more than the man. The advancing group consisted of an old woman, very evidently a *grande dame* from her dress and manner—supported on each side by a young and good-looking Irish girl—evidently her maids. In addition to the support lent by their round, fat arms the old lady leaned heavily on a stick, which she pushed ahead of her with each feeble step. The ferrule of the stick was loose, and as it slid along the hard floor it gave out a curious reedy note.

Suddenly, and for no reason apparent to the intruder, the progress of the nice old lady was interrupted by the man in the corner. First he held up one hand; then he rapped sharply on the floor with an impatient foot, at which the two maids looked at their frail little charge with a touch of tenderness and slowly turned her about-face; and again they retreated beyond the angle of vision of the looker-on, but only for a second.

The rasping note of the cane sliding across the floor was resumed, and the three started once more for the distant table, this time the stubby old man in the corner rising with much graciousness to receive the old lady from the arms of her two youthful guardians and thanking them with a courteous gesture. He placed the old lady in her chair, sat down himself and began speaking, accompanying his words with gestures every shade of which, even to the uncurling of his fine fingers, seemed a bit of art in itself.

Grimsy could not distinguish the words; but, as he listened, fascinated at the queer sight on which he had stumbled—with no qualms of conscience—he thought this voice must be the most beautiful in all the world. An almost metrical cadence with which the speaker accented his phrases, and the timbre, as vibrant and resonant as the G string of a violin, reached the listener like a far-away song one might hear in a dream.

As the old lady raised her face to the speaker and, for the first time, the light of the lamp fell full on her features, Grimsy started. He knew the face; but the shock of its suddenly flashing on his vision in this strange quarter of the city scattered his wits, so that he could not for the life of him place it. He only knew he had seen that face in the newspapers many times; and the incomplete recollection brought with it an impression of something sweet and good. She belonged to his coterie of newspaper friends. And whatever it may have been he had read of her, it was something nice. Certainly the real face before him now suggested something to be venerated by all who looked on it—old age come to its own beautifully.

His curious attention to this scene was roughly wrenched loose by a cackling laugh from a table nearer the door—a table he had not noticed in his interest in the old lady. As he looked at the merry one he rubbed his eyes. He was poorly prepared for the surprise. It was none other than Mr. Andrew Carnegie, if Grimsy knew Andrew Carnegie—and he was positive he could pick the diminutive ironmaster in a million. And Mr. Carnegie was engaged in the most cordial, though somewhat guarded, conversation with Mr. John D. Rockefeller!

If young Grimsy had not been such a close student of current events and personalities in the newspapers he would have pinched himself and crept away at this juncture; but Grimsy did nothing of the kind. In his eagerness he polished the dusty glass transom with his glove to get a better view of the scene which now fairly had his hair standing on end, each follicle counting itself root by root. The two multimillionaires were at dinner. The ironmaster helped himself from a bottle. Grimsy had read only recently words from the lips of Mr. Carnegie himself to the effect that he and Emperor Wilhelm had one habit in common, that of taking a half glass of liquor with their meals; but Grimsy had no idea that the jolly little ironmaster referred to a glass of this size. It was an eight-ounce tumbler.

Mr. Carnegie wrapped his leg—which only reached the first rung of his chair—about the spindles, and, as he quaffed from the goblet—without watering the stuff—he manipulated his merry little eyes in the most surprising manner. Evidently the talk had to do with a toupee Mr. Rockefeller wore. Mr. Rockefeller did wear a toupee, and his companion's eyes pointed very plainly to the fact that the wig was somewhat one-sided for the moment, disclosing at one corner a bald pate as shiny as a billiard ball.

At this moment an untoward incident interrupted the amazing panorama of which Mr. Moberly Grimsy had been so fortunate as to have a peep on this night of nights. He had risen on tiptoe in his excitement. He overbalanced himself; the door gave easily; and before he could recover himself he fell headlong into the room.

A shriek of many voices punctuated his crash to the floor—then dead silence; then sudden darkness, filled with the scamperings of many feet. Heavy hands laid hold of him so he could not move; and a voice, bell-like in its intonation, addressed a question to some one near him in the dark:

"Where is Bannon? Isn't he out in front?"

And then some one replied in an impersonal tone: "No; I sent him down to Murray's an hour ago."

That was all—a few words exchanged in the darkness, seemingly apropos of nothing in particular, least of all of the squirming form of young Moberly Grimsy, which they were holding in their midst.

"Let me go!" cried the young man, attempting to strike out with his feet, only to find that his feet, too, were fast. "I came here—looking—for a place to—Quit that! Take your thumb—"

A thumb was doing its best to dislocate his Adam's apple, and a hand over his mouth cut off further remarks from Mr. Moberly Grimsy. He was gently picked off the floor by four men—one at each quarter—in silence. They might have been his pallbearers, so solemnly did they start off with their burden, the hand over his mouth now being supplanted by a handkerchief jammed down his gullet. They turned this way and that. The hollow echoes of their footfalls and the crowding of the men carrying him told him they were threading a tunnel, though evidently not the same magic gate by which he had been permitted to enter on the unsuspecting assemblage.

He wondered whither they were taking him. Suddenly the dull sounds of the living city that had always been in his ears became louder, like stage thunder, and a breath of cool air told him he was in a street. A coat was over his head now, so he could not see. He was gently set on the flagging of the curb; and then in an electric fraction of a second the coat was gone, the gag was gone and his pallbearers had vanished.

He got to his feet and found himself rubbing his head and surveying a dimly lit avenue that presented no familiar landmarks. The thing had occurred so quickly that now, as he looked round in the dim light and found himself alone, it was quite simple to persuade himself that it was all some lurid fabrication of his brain. He walked to the end of the block and looked at the lamppost. It said Jane Street on one side. Some small boy had put a stone through the glass legend on the other side, so the intersecting street remained a mystery.

He walked back through the street, trying to fix on the house that had emitted him a few moments before, but all the houses—old-fashioned brick structures, ornamented with iron grilles at doors and windows—looked out cheerlessly and impersonally.

Suddenly Moberly Grimsy broke into a run. He must find somebody, because the strangest idea had come into his mind, which, while he fuddled over his whereabouts, seemed to have been working subconsciously at something else. Two blocks farther on he encountered a young man, swinging a cane, emerging from a side street. Grimsy did not stand on ceremony.

"Isn't it a fact," he cried, bringing the young man to a sudden stop by the simple expedient of stepping in front of him, "isn't it a fact that John D. Rockefeller was playing golf at his home in Cleveland, Ohio, this morning, and that he beat the bogey?"

The young man looked at him for a second before replying. Then he said:

"My acquaintance with Mr. Rockefeller is confined to the interesting gossip of his doings as set forth in the newspapers. And," he said with a smile, "with that authority I think I can assure you that Mr. Rockefeller indeed was in Cleveland this morning. I recollect an item to that effect in an afternoon edition which I saw but an hour ago."

"Then how," began Moberly Grimsy, squaring off and holding up one handful of fingers to count off the points of his argument, "how in the name of the seven sins could I have seen him hobnobbing with

Mr. Carnegie less than half an hour ago, and within one hundred yards of this spot?"

"It is rather remarkable," said the other soothingly. "Come! Are you going in my direction? We will try to figure it out together as we walk along."

Grimsy came to his senses. He tried to laugh, to excuse himself for this sudden attack of his on a stranger—a stranger who seemed very much of a gentleman from the manner in which he had met the situation.

"Show me how to get out of this hole, if you will," said Grimsy. "My mind is giving way. I have just gone through a most amazing experience; in fact, I am not quite sure—I am lost!" he said, breaking suddenly in on his disjointed sentences. "If you will be kind enough to direct me I will not further trespass on your good nature."

"I will do better than that," said the stranger, taking him by the arm. "It is but a step to New York. I am going there myself."

And indeed it was but a step. Under the guidance of the skilled pilot the tangles of off-shooting streets straightened out and they set foot in Sixth Avenue as unexpectedly to Grimsy as one comes on a hidden pond in the Maine woods. Grimsy turned round and surveyed the entrance to the New York he knew.

"I was looking for an out-of-the-way place to eat," he explained; and then abruptly: "I thank you. I will not intrude further on your good nature. You must think me loony; but, believe me—"

His guide held up a slender gloved hand and smiled deprecatingly.

"If you have not yet dined," he said, "let us make it a company of two. I have leisure—and an appetite. Possibly I can be of service to you."

The stranger looked at his companion out of shrewd gray eyes. Some restless spirit within was clamoring for adventure, and the occasion seemed to promise something of the sort surely. He led Grimsy, the latter protesting weakly, to Fifth Avenue, and there, a block to the north, turned into a mullioned doorway of brownstone, where they were instantly greeted by a gorgeous person, evidently a *maitre d'hotel,* much rigged up for his part. His guide seemed a person of consequence; and Grimsy, impressed, followed on through the heavily carpeted hall to a small room hung with deep curtains and warmed by a glowing fire on a stone hearth.

"May I be permitted to suggest the *filet de sole,* M'sieu Godahl?" said the *maitre d'hotel* in French as he seated them.

"Godahl!" cried the youth ecstatically. "Are you indeed Godahl?"

It was indeed Godahl whom chance had thrown in the way of the distressed Grimsy; and the latter, whose one-sided friendships were all gathered through the common medium of the press, impulsively seized that arch-rogue by the hand in an outburst of enthusiasm. Did not the reading public know this Godahl as one of the institutions of the town? As a matter of fact the infallible thief, in his assumed character of a well-found young man-about-town, had proved it impossible to keep his picturesque personality from the eyes of prying newsgatherers and camera men; and he was known outside of the favored circle to which he belonged as Godahl—just Godahl, as one knows Matty, or Corot, or Napoleon, or Fatima. The name Godahl was an established entity.

So, before the clams were gone—little clams the size of a dime— Moberly Grimsy had launched himself spontaneously into a confession, glowing with the subtle fire of a well-flattered person, a condition of mind that some personages have the faculty of conferring on those about them.

Godahl studied his man as he gave attention to the strange story. Godahl was partial to this man Grimsy's type—closely cropped red hair; freckles; tawny eyes; and a natural manner of wearing clothes— even though those clothes were obviously ready made.

"The woman!" said Godahl. "The old lady—tell me more about her. You say you know her. Who was she?"

"Who was the woman," said Grimsy, bringing together the leading strings of recollection, "who furnished the money necessary to buy that island in the Gulf of Mexico for the protection of migrating shore birds?"

"Mrs. Jeremiah Trigg," responded Godahl; and the restless fingers of that master craftsman ceased caressing the thin stem of his glass.

"Ai! yi! Mrs. Jeremiah Trigg!" exclaimed young Grimsy; and he stared at his companion, interpreting the sudden calm that had come over Godahl for lack of interest. It was, as a matter of fact, the reverse.

Jeremiah Trigg had run out a life of seventy-odd years in the character of what Wall Street was pleased to call a shark. His main occupation was loans—call loans; but, using the genius that evidenced itself to the world only as brittle sensibilities and fingers that stuck to gold, he had steered the ship of several great family fortunes for the younger generations—and the best evidence of his genius lay in the fact that these same fortunes had begun to disintegrate soon after his death. His character, to the public who were never permitted to peep behind the scenes, was that of a miser hard as nails, with a heart wrung dry of pity. Yet at his death he had consecrated his fortune of some seventy million dollars to simple charity—not for himself, that his abused name might be acclaimed, but for his widow, the gentle wife whom all the world had revered. The fortune was deeded by the will to no other trust than her kindly sympathies.

And immediately on her assuming the responsibilities of the administration of great wealth she had been hounded by an importunate army of professional charity-mongers—implored; besought; threatened in the name of pity, justice, patriotism and all the other masks of the nefarious crew who ply the profession of leeching on charity. At length the kind creature, who loved nothing so much as simple home life and an open, unaffected communion with the whole world, was forced into a seclusion that could be compared only to that of some prisoner rescued from a howling mob by his keepers; until she was forced to bury herself under a cloud of retainers to fight off the importunities of the world she would have loved to succor in her own sweet way.

"And this man?" pursued Godahl, thrilling. "You tell me that when she started across the floor he rapped her back and made her try it again."

"Yes."

"Describe him."

"A head like—like Daniel Webster! Magnificent! Enormous shoulders—long arms; and his hands—the best way I can describe them is that they seemed to float in the air as he gesticulated."

"And a voice like a god?" said Godahl, suddenly leaning forward over the table. "A voice like a god, eh?"

"God? Yes!" cried Grimsy. "Such a voice as I never—"

Godahl, however, was not listening to him as the young man rattled on in a maze of hyperbole. Godahl had risen to his feet and was pacing the room.

"I am going to trust you," he said, suddenly coming to a stop in front of Moberly Grimsy and putting a hand on his shoulder. "I never saw you before in my life, and your interest in the golf score of John D. Rockefeller was not, I should say, a propitious opening for a prolonged friendship. Listen to me! You are a bank clerk, you say, at the Cheltenham Bank. Forget that. Marston, the vice-president, will give me the loan of you.

"Grimsy," said Godahl, dragging up a chair and sitting down at the corner of the table, "the greatest actor the world has ever known is a man who has never been on the stage! And his name is David Hartmann. A mind like a diamond, a voice of a god—and the frame of a hideous gorilla! That's Hartmann. Embittered, unscrupulous. Think, man! A man with the wits of an oaf has the world at his feet at the Metropolitan Opera House to-night because the good God above gave him not only a throat but the physique of a man. The lack of a body of the most commonplace proportion, such as you and I and everybody else possess as an inalienable right, is all that prevents the greatest master of his art in this generation from claiming his own. Tell me, could the lithe Hamlet stalk the stage in the guise of a hideous ape! Imagine Lear seizing his straws and crying, 'Ay, every inch a king!' if he were a spindle-legged dwarf!

"Enough of this!" cried Godahl, suddenly rescuing himself from his thoughts. "Never mind about your precious cage at the bank. You are mine! There is work to be done."

VII

Old Fifth Avenue is gone, and gone forever. There is a fringe along the edge of Washington Square and for a few blocks to the north still stubbornly holding out against the encroachment of trade to suggest the stately solidarity of the aristocracy of this quarter a generation ago. There is a zone now given over to sweatshops; and from Twenty-third Street north stretches the Rue de la Paix of this side of the water, advancing its half-mile each year with glittering windows. They say it shall not encroach north of the park; but it is already there, clamoring at the barrier.

As with the lower end of the Avenue, this region of superrefined trade to the north still harbors in its midst, stubbornly refusing to move, some examples of the fine old brownstone mansions that gave the Avenue its old-time distinction. Such a one is to be found just above the zone where the crosstown flood at Forty-second Street disputes the right-of-way with the north and south streams of vehicles and pedestrians. Strangers to New York know it to-day probably better than New Yorkers themselves, for the reason that the so-called seeing-the-city automobiles, which make this a regular route daily, are always somewhat boisterous when passing the spot. The megaphone man, as noisy as some fishwife at the town pump retailing choice bits of scandal about the great and near great, raises his trumpet at this point and announces in tones to be heard on the pavement on both sides:

"In the mansion on your left, ladies and gentlemen, you see the old-time residence of the late Jeremiah Trigg!"

The name is quite sufficient. Instantly the rubberneck audience begins to titter and to recount to each other the eccentricities of this famous old put-and-call shark of Wall Street. These stories, for a period of many years, flooded the press of the country; and the public, like our friend Moberly Grimsy, makes its friends and accumulates its enemies through the newspapers. In this old house the man who lived for a principle and died happy in the consciousness of having confided the administration of his principle to sure hands spent fifty years of his life. Behind these windows, hung with rich tapestries, he sat in the evening with his wife, playing with the family cat and a ball of yarn. When he had something nice to suggest to his good wife to do for other people he was too shy to tell her, and the family cat became the medium of his confidence, his plans being expressed in a loud voice clearly audible to the good wife who sat by knitting.

There was a little rag doll, loaded with shot, which sat on the floor and listened with wide-open eyes as the cat played unheeding through the unfolding of gorgeous plans to make some one—or many, many ones—happy without knowing the source of that happiness. The doll had a duty in life quite as dignified as that of the cat—its duty being to sit tight against the library door, so that the door might not swing shut on its hinges and shut off the coziness of the other room.

Uncle Jeremiah, so they jocosely called him downtown, discussed the hopes and fears and tears of their farmers—the old couple counted many countrymen to whom their bounty was more generous than that of the stubborn soil—much as if they had been sitting before a fire in some rude farmhouse and the cares of the neighborhood were theirs to alleviate with the simplest of godly alms, instead of a complex machinery that every moment must protect itself from lying greed.

Here in the evening was always the picture of home—a home that is being banished from the many palaces along the way; a home that was not only sufficient unto its own peace and happiness but which radiated warm beneficence to many other homes.

This evening—the evening following that on which Moberly Grimsy at last found a sociable friend at table—the picture was the same, except that Uncle Jeremiah was gone on his long journey. There was an open fire in the deep grate; outside was the soft coming of evening and gently falling snow. The old lady sat knitting; the big-eyed doll was thinking of the most serious things of life at its post by the door; and the cat, the same cat, languidly studied the ball of yarn, wondering whether, as a matter of fact, it was not getting too old to be frisking this foolish thing about the room.

The servants were coming and going on tiptoe over the soft, padded carpets, exchanging words in whispers—mysterious whispers, accompanied by smiles that signified that something of moment was afoot.

The butler, who had been with the family since they came to town, in his present graduate capacity was directing the maneuvers from the seclusion of the street hall, out of sight of the old lady. He was whispering to the second butler that the second-in-command was to be in command of this ship—information that had been explained with stolid iteration through many busy days now—days that were busy, but with their business concealed under smooth machinery.

The clock on the mantel struck the hour of four. The old lady roused herself with a sigh and looked up with a smile when two plump Irish girls approached and helped her to her feet, and muffled her in wraps of downiest texture. She took her cane; and, with an arm on each side to support her, she made her way to the door where, as if by the magic of some hidden stage director, four secretaries were in waiting. They were, in fact, the bodyguard. They were needed. As the door opened a little man with a greasy black beard, who had been in waiting at the curb, dashed up the steps and attempted to push past the advance guard. He held a paper in his hand, and he cried, as a secretary held him off:

"It is most worthy, madam. I could convince you if I could have but a word with you."

"Mrs. Trigg receives no strangers on account of her advanced years," explained the secretary politely; and as the party passed down the steps, he successfully blocked the charity seeker from his prey.

The attendants surrounded the old woman like a cloud. There were other importunate ones at the curb; but so closely did the guard cling that they had no opportunity to voice their harsh claims on the bounty of this poor creature. It was always thus. The army studied the habits of this household like a hawk, hovering about the mansion at all hours of the day.

"Did you get a good view of her?" asked Godahl.

"Yes," said young Grimsy. "I saw her perfectly. It is she, I am certain." The pair had sauntered up just in time to witness the disgraceful exhibition that was a daily occurrence now. "Did you notice her cane?" said Grimsy.

Godahl had not, he said.

"The ferrule was loose and made a queer noise, like the low string on a violin, when she pushed it across the pavement. It was the same cane she used the other night."

"Delightful," said Godahl. "Now we shall see whether the rest of the drama is played according to the cards."

It was an hour later when the two sauntered along the Avenue just as the returning carriage of Mrs. Jeremiah Trigg drew up at a brownstone house. It was the same carriage, but not the same brownstone house as before.

The same curtains—apparently—hung at the windows; the same mellow radiance of the table lamp and the flickering light of the fire played on the tapestries; the same butler waited at the top of the steps; the same cat and doll guarded inside; and the same coterie of guards, men and maids, inclosed the figure of Mrs. Jeremiah Trigg as she crossed the pavement.

The house occupied the same position in the block—but it was not the same block; the location was half a mile to the north. It was the new home of Mrs. Jeremiah Trigg. Trade, clamoring at her doors, had so far encroached on the old home that it was thought advisable by the family council of lawyers to move the old lady—and to move her room by room without any suspicion on her part that she was being moved.

Some day, if she did not discover the illusion herself, those servants who loved her as blood kin would tell her of their carefully planned ruse. To-night she took up her knitting beside the silver-framed picture of Uncle Jerry on the table, blissfully unconscious that even the unbalanced door had been doctored to a degree of verisimilitude that would have deceived far sharper eyes than hers.

It was at ten sharp the next morning that the chief clerk of Vice-President Marston, of the Cheltenham Bank, handed the latter the telephone with the information that some one wished to speak to him from the Trigg home. Uncle Jerry had dominated the affairs of this bank during his lifetime and the widow retained control through her attorneys.

"This is Martin speaking," said a voice on the wire. Martin was one of the many secretaries who hovered about the old lady.

"Hello, Charlie! How are you? From this distance I should say you have a frog in your throat," said the genial banker.

"That's not worrying me half so much as other people's troubles," said the husky voice, with a cough. "The old lady wants those bronze medallions that are in the big strongbox, and there is nothing to do but to bring the whole box up here to the house."

"Humph! Well, in your case, I should advise calling out the Seventy-first Regiment for a bodyguard," said the jocose banker.

"Thanks! I am going to pass the buck to you. The old lady wants you to bring it up yourself. Ha-ha!"

And so it was that the banker found himself, half an hour later, sitting in a closed automobile, with two big bank guards and an imposing-looking steel box, and bound, not unhappily at that— because the dangers of the city streets did not daunt him—for "Uncle Jerry Trigg's house," as he had instructed the driver. As the car came to a stop at the curb he sprang out and up the steps, waiting at the door, opened by the second man, for his two guards to bring in their precious burden.

"Mr. Martin, sir," said the man, "asked me to tell you that he was called out to the Sunnyside meeting and would not be able to see you, sir."

As Marston handed his hat and coat to the man he nodded casually to two young men who were passing through the hall to the rear of the first floor. The whisking of a white apron about the turn of the stairs indicated the presence of one of the Irish maids.

"This house smells good!" exclaimed the banker to himself, as though he had stumbled on a new source of happiness on this visit. He looked into the drawing-room, but retreated immediately, his finger to his lips to enjoin silence on the two men who were depositing their burden. The old lady, her knitting fallen to the floor, was asleep in her chair. The cat sat purring before the fire; the rag doll, of all the room, seemed the only thing alive, and it sat staring accusingly at him with its big eyes.

As he took in the scene something in him welled up and overflowed. It was the memory of just such a scene long, long ago when he was a boy, and the recollection came on him with a rush of warmth and tenderness. He tiptoed to a chair and sat down quietly, signaling to his men to place their burden in the doorway and withdraw as quietly as possible.

Now the old lady stirred herself uneasily, sighed, and opened her eyes. For a moment she did not see him, but smiled at the old cat stretching itself in the extravagant manner of a languorous feline before the warm glow of the fire. Everything in the room seemed to rouse itself with her. Her eyes came with a start to the figure of Marston, who rose and came forward.

"Don't move!" he cried, smiling and reaching out his hands to implore her to remain seated; but she rose to her feet and pushed the cane ahead of her. She permitted him to help her to her seat again, and she sat holding his hard hand between her two withered hands and looking out the window. It was a silence he dared not break, though it made him uncomfortable. It was broken at last by the approach of the second man bearing tea things. At eleven every day Mrs. Jeremiah Trigg had her tea and her cat was given a bit of cheese to nibble. Mrs. Trigg in talking about cats used to say that she ascribed the faithfulness of her cats to their eleven-o'clock cheese.

Marston had come with his expectations made up for a brisk chat with the old lady; but it turned out to be rather a trying situation for him. She cried softly throughout the time they sat before the tray— crying softly as old women cry when they spin the thread of memories that are dearest to them. He made one or two ineffectual attempts to say something; but his efforts ended so lamely that he gave it up and it was with great relief that he heard the approaching footsteps of the servant.

"Madam is—madam is in one of her moods—thinking—to-day. You understand, sir," said the second man in his ear.

Marston looked up and the man averted his eyes quickly. Marston nodded his head. He rose and drew off to a corner with the man.

"I understand," he said. "If the world only knew Uncle Jerry as we remember him!"

The man nodded vigorously and seemed about to cry.

"Will she sign for this or will one of the secretaries come?" asked the bank official, indicating the box.

"I think she will, as they are the bronze medallions she wishes and she wants to find them herself. I will see, sir."

The man stepped to the side of the old lady and whispered to her. She looked up and nodded vigorously, smiling through her tears.

"Oh, you understand, Thomas, don't you?" she said. "Ah, I shall be so happy when we are together again! There—there! Why should we torture you young people?" And she dragged her eyes back from the fire, and, with trembling hand, wrote her signature.

Marston made his adieux as quickly as possible. The man opened the door for him and, seeing two men in conversation with the bank guards, who stood at the curb waiting orders, drew back hurriedly and said:

"Are they friends of yours, sir? We must be very careful, as so many people are ready to take advantage of the old lady."

"You don't need to worry about them," said Marston, laughing; for he recognized in the two men Worden, the managing head of the Bankers' Protective Association for the Metropolitan district, and young Moberly Grimsy. The man inside was still peering through the interstices of the ground-glass carving of the door as Marston went down the steps.

"What are you two doing in this neck of the woods? I thought you were on your vacation, Grimsy, with that young devil Godahl."

"This house is pinched," said Worden, starting up the steps with a laugh, as he ran his arm through the banker's and turned him back. "I have been waiting for you to come out, to have a good look at your face when the ceiling comes down on your head." So saying he touched the bell. He looked through the glass of the door impudently. "Run, you terrier!" he chuckled; and he raised his heavy cane and shattered the glass of the door. "Tell Captain McCarthy he had better bring up his men and throw them across on both sides. The whole town will be here in another five minutes!" he said, turning and addressing a man in the street who was off at a sharp run.

The astonished Marston saw a patrol wagon round the corner emptying itself in a jiffy. People in the street had already begun to gather in front of the house, attracted by the sound of the broken glass and the sudden appearance of the policemen in force.

Worden had run his hand inside the door and slipped the lock. Marston, shivering, followed him, with young Grimsy close at his heels. The parlor was empty, save for the cat and the rag doll. The old lady was gone; the steel box was gone; and the second man was nowhere in sight.

The banker stared about him.

Worden and Grimsy looked at him soberly for a moment, but the strain was too much for them and they broke into shouts of mirth. The color gradually returned to his face and his knees again showed signs of behaving themselves under this kind of attack. If that box was gone and gone beyond recovery—whatever might be the explanation of this weird situation—Marston concluded that the superintendent of the Bankers' Protective Association would be laughing on the other side of his mouth.

"For the love of the holies, don't stand there grinning at me as though I were a lunatic! Tell me—what does it all mean?" cried the amazed banker.

"Come with us," said Worden, showing no desire for haste or inclination for any other task than relieving the curiosity of his friend. He took Marston by the arm and the three marched upstairs. The bedroom floor above the parlor was empty—bare-floored. So was the third floor and the servants' quarters above. So was the basement floor. With the exception of the parlor floor the house was stripped to the very walls.

"But—Mrs. Trigg! Where has she gone?" cried Marston when he had convinced himself.

"I don't know, I am sure," said Worden. "Mrs. Trigg hasn't been in this house in twenty hours, to my knowledge."

"Hasn't been in the house, you idiot! Then whom, pray, have I been taking tea with in this room—not ten minutes ago?"

"Marston," said Worden, "you have been entertained for the last quarter of an hour or so by a stock company composed of some of the most distinguished actors and actresses out of jail. Mrs. Trigg was moved out of this house yesterday and the furniture of this room was shifted to her new home just above Fifty-second Street before she returned from her drive. With the connivance of a rascally second butler the cleverest gang of thieves this side of the River Jordan rigged up the rooms again for your especial entertainment this morning. And I suspect," he said, glancing slyly at young Grimsy, "that if it had not been for Grimsy here, and his friend Godahl, you would now be poorer by the several hundred thousand dollars' worth of bonds that steel box contained.

"Come!" he cried with a laugh, as he snapped his fingers in Marston's ears—for that person was standing transfixed like one in a trance—"I'll take you behind the scenes if you want to see the rest of the show."

The three went to the garden in the rear of the house. In one corner, handcuffed, snarling and defiant, stood the second butler, the key of the combination. In another corner were three women—two of them girls made up for the parts of the two Irish maids, and the third the old woman; who had entertained Marston with tea and tears so effectively. The girls were in a state of collapse ; but the woman, amazing in her makeup for the part even now when she had lost her countenance, stared boldly at them. In the basement were the two young men who had masqueraded as secretaries.

"I congratulate you, madam," said Marston, now quite himself again. "Your talents are worthy of better things—believe me!"

"You needn't inform her as to her talents," said Worden. "That woman is Mary Mannerley. We used to think she was the greatest emotional actress that ever lived, back in the seventies. Lord! Until I found she was in this game I thought she was dead and buried. The rascals dragged her out of an old folks' home for the part."

Marston shook his head, bewildered.

"You ought to see the bunch we just nailed downtown at the restaurant," cried Worden:

"There was John D., and Andy Carnegie, and—Gad! Tom, when I first laid eyes on the bunch an hour ago I swear I couldn't tell at first whether I had stumbled into a meeting of the directors of the Steel Trust or Mrs. Jarley's Waxworks!"

"Would you be surprised," said Godahl, taking the arm of a man in the crowd that surged about the police lines, "would you be surprised if I should ask you to accompany me?"

The man he addressed was less than five feet tall, though he had the head and shoulders of a giant. The massive head turned slowly and regarded the speaker. Godahl's manner was, to all appearances, friendly. He was smiling and his tone was casual, so that none of the crowd, eager to seize on a morsel of excitement outside, turned to look in his direction.

The small man regarded Godahl steadily under his gray brows. "What a grand old warlock it is!" thought Godahl.

"I should not be surprised," said the man in clear, bell-like tones. "If you will indicate the way I shall be pleased to follow. Or will you permit me to precede you?"

Godahl turned and shouldered his way out of the crowd; and on the outskirts he was joined by the man with the ludicrous body and the Jovian head. They strode along side by side. Clearly, thought Godahl, David Hartmann considered himself under arrest. The old man had been absent when the police raided the meeting-place downtown, and as a member of the crowd had watched the fiasco of his great plan here in front of the mansion that his great brain had furnished and peopled with play-actors and properties. He had again escaped them.

"I am sorry to have spoiled your scene," said Godahl as they swung along together. "I have been watching you for three years, Hartmann. Ha-ha! That was beautiful when you gave that chorus-girl dinner to Senator Newstead in Chicago."

A year before the whole country had been convulsed at the circumstantial tale of a gay dinner in the public dining-room of the Auditorium at which Senator Newstead, candidate for governor on the Republican ticket, was the apparent host. The pious old senator bitterly denounced the calumny; but there were plenty of witnesses to swear that it was really he, and he was snowed under at the polls.

"I could stand for that and bless you for it, Hartmann," went on Godahl; "and the Blackburn case, and the Hamilton affair; but when you come to tamper with the comfort and happiness of a woman who has paid the penalty of martyrdom simply for being good and doing good, I step in and say No! I didn't know you had shifted to New York until my redheaded friend fell in on your rehearsal the other night."

"The redheaded boy—yes," said David Hartmann to himself though aloud, and carving his words with that devilish trick of enunciation he alone possessed. "Yes, I thought so. My man," he added, indicating Godahl though he did not deign to turn his head in the direction of the young man, "I do not believe I care to discuss the matter with you. I am presuming that you have authority to ask me to accompany you."

"No," said Godahl with the consciousness of a bitter taste in his mouth. "I am taking you to the Grand Central Station to see you aboard any train you may elect to choose. See—we are here now. I have money. It is yours. Even now the police of the country are seeking you. Your mates will squeal—that's absolute. I am ready to aid you in any way I can—not because of to-day, but because of —"

Godahl ran his fingers through the air in front of him impatiently.

"You are not of the police, then—or with authority to detain me?"

Passers-by turned their heads to catch the nuances of that voice, though the words were low. Godahl shook his head.

"No?" said the voice.

"No," said Godahl.

David Hartmann came to a stop and raised his hand—that hand which Moberly Grimsy said seemed to float in the air. He waved it at a policeman who stood on the corner. The policeman came to his side and bent over.

"You do not know me, my man," he said. "I am David Hartmann. That means nothing to you. The police seek me. I am wanted for robbery. I might tear my soul to shreds in hopeless flight; but I am marked. See—my ridiculous little legs! My friend," he said, turning to Godahl and taking him by the hand, "I do not know who you may be, but I thank you. If I did not so love this bitter life I might have the courage to die; but I have not the courage."

That voice, ringing like a knell, sang in his ears as Godahl hurried across town.

"What would a few hundred thousand dollars in gold bonds more or less have meant to the old lady anyway?" he cried suddenly to himself as he stopped and called a hansom. "Nothing! Bah!"

The End

CPSIA information can be obtained
at www.ICGtesting.com
Printed in the USA
LVOW11s0109120318
569488LV00001BA/8/P